The Alpha's Broken Luna

Lillith Mykals Kennedy

Published by Lillith Mykals Kennedy, 2022.

THE ALPHA'S BROKEN LUNA

First edition. December 2, 2022.

ISBN: 979-8215459355

Written by Lillith Mykals Kennedy.

Chapter 1- My Wedding

Kayla POV

I never thought there would be so much fanfare over my little wedding. Soran and I are both so young and full of life. He is perfect for me, and I am perfect for him.

No, we are not mates, but we can grow to love one another. He is good to me, and my parents adore him. This union will combine our packs as he becomes Alpha, and I become his Luna tonight. His Alpha ceremony and our wedding ceremony here with my pack and his to celebrate will be the most amazing night of our lives.

I cannot wait to start a life with Alpha Soran. I never thought I would be a Luna. Now, I am marrying a wonderful wolf at a dream wedding. It is unbelievable. Unfortunately, his brother cannot be here. He is an Alpha for a pack in the north. I can meet his brother later.

"Kayla, your dress has arrived," Candy, my sweet sister, says as she rushes into my room. Candy has loved every moment of planning my wedding.

It seems like everything came together perfectly. Well, almost everything. Another Alpha asked for my hand, but I refused him. He became very angry.

When my father made the announcement that I would be looking for a mate, several wolves courted me. I chose Soran because he is kind and closer to my age. Alpha Ranon is older than me, and he seemed angry. I only needed to marry someone that could help protect our pack.

Our pack is small. Most of the younger pack members have moved on to other packs, and now we are mostly elders or young women that will marry and leave. I had to help my pack, and that is why I agreed not to seek my mate.

Lucky for me, Soran reached out to my father. He showed interest early. We agreed to marry and be true to one another. I care for him deeply, and I believe that the two of us will grow to love one another.

"Thanks, sis. Is mother coming to help me get in my dress?" I ask Candy.

She shakes her head. "She is swamped with guests. I cannot believe how big Soran's pack is. What about the brother? Is he coming? I want to see what he looks like," Candy says.

I help Candy place my dress bag on the bed. "Alpha Marcus is married, but we will meet him eventually. He has a younger brother, Alpha Maximus," I tease her.

Candy looks genuinely worried for me. I sit down beside my dress bag, take my sister's hand and pull her to sit beside me. "What is it, sis?" I ask her.

Big tears begin to roll down her face. "I am worried about you. It is not fair for you to give up on a mate," Candy cries.

I rub the top of her hand. "Soran is a good wolf, and he will be a wonderful husband and father. Just imagine our life. I will be his Luna, and we will have a big house with kids, and it will be everything I have ever wanted," I try to explain to her.

"But he is not your mate," Candy says.

"I am fine with it. Please be fine with it. Saving our pack is the most important thing to me," I say. I reach over and wipe the tears away from Candy's eyes. I pull her into my arms.

"I love you," Candy says.

"I love you too," I say to her.

"Now, no more crying. I have to get ready for my larger-than-life wedding," I say. Candy gets up and looks out my bedroom window. Her eyes are huge as she looks out over the people gathering.

"It is unbelievable. I cannot remember the last time there were this many wolves here. It is wild. Maybe I will meet someone tonight. I am old enough to find my mate," Candy says.

"Mom would die if you left her too. Try to wait a little while, so she has at least one daughter still in the house," I say.

Candy gives me a crazy look. "Fine," she says.

"Okay, so stop trying to find your mate and help me get into this dress, please," I say.

Candy unzips my dress bag. We both look at the dress and smile at each other. "I want to wear it when I get married," Candy says.

"It is yours at the end of the night," I say to her. We are both star-struck by the details that Hannah put into my dress.

Hannah, our mother's oldest friend, took our mother's wedding dress and made me a new wedding dress. She sewed the smallest stitches of our pack and Soran's pack symbols onto the dress. The ivory dress looks like something for a beautiful fairy queen.

My mother comes into the bedroom to see the two of us looking at the dress. "It is unbelievable," my mother says.

"Candy wants it for her wedding," I say, still in awe looking at the beauty in front of me.

"Well, you cannot get married unless you put it on, Kayla," my mother says.

"Right. Are you staying to help?" I ask her.

She smiles at me and shakes her head no. " I have to entertain our guest. You will learn the ropes of a Luna soon enough, my sweet girl," my mother says.

She is right. I will be married to Soran tonight. I will be his Luna.

"What is it?" Candy asks me.

"I am marrying an Alpha, and I am going to be a Luna. I am so happy," I say.

"Well, first, we have to get you in this dress," Candy says. I step into the dress, and Candy does the hard part. She pulls it up and ties it as I look in the mirror, watching as I become the Luna bride of Alpha Soran.

"This day could not be any more perfect," I say.

Chapter 2 – Alpha Ranon

Luna Kayla POV

I cannot believe how fast his Alpha Ceremony and our wedding went. It seems like it flew by as I was looking into his heavenly eyes. I hoped that I would feel the calling of my mate when we married and that he would be my mate after all. It did not happen, and I am okay with that. Alpha Soran is so kind toward me that I can live with being his wife no matter what.

The wolf council whisks him away from me. His mother and father take me to introduce me to everyone. It pains me that I will never remember all of these names. Cousins, uncles, aunts, inlaws, and more wolves are saying hi and congratulating me on my wedding. I am overwhelmed, to say the least, as I meet and greet each of them.

I look over my shoulder as the wolf council and Alpha Soran stands before us. They are shooting fireworks into the sky. Alpha Soran is smiling at me, and I feel the most fantastic feeling inside me. I am happy. Our eyes stay locked for a moment, and then I see him. Alpha Ranon is here and his wolves; none of them look happy. This intrusion is not good.

My small tribe of wolves begins to scatter. The elders are no match for Alpha Ranon and his men. I look to Alpha Soran. I do not know what to do. Alpha Ranon and his men are slaughtering us, all of us, as he makes his way toward me. It all happens so fast. My ears are ringing from the sounds of screaming, and there is a fire. Something is on fire.

"Mother, Candy, Father," I scream out, but everyone is running and trying to get away from Alpha Ranon and his ruthless men.

"Luna Kayla!" I look to see Alpha Soran trying to get to me, his warriors are fighting, but there are so many wolves with Alpha Ranon. His pack is too much for us. We will all die.

"RUN!" Alpha Soran screams for me to run, but I will not leave without my parents and my sister. I search frantically for my parents.

I find them together, dead. He killed my parents all because I refused him. Why? I have to find my sister.

"Candy!" I scream out to her. I feel someone run up behind me and grab me. I kick and scream as I fight to get away from whoever has me.

"I have her," a rough voice growls. The wolf takes me to the same platform I said I do to Alpha Soran. He puts me on my knees. I look up to see Alpha Ranon.

"You should have chosen me, bitch," Alpha Ranon says to me. He kicks me in the face, and another wolf sits me back on my knees. When I open my eyes, I see Alpha Soran and my sister.

"Which one do you want to live?" Alpha Ranon asks me.

I look at him, puzzled. "What?" I ask him.

"One can live, and one can die, so which one?" he asks me.

"Kill me, let her sister live," Alpha Soran says.

"Very well," Alpha Ranon says.

"NOOOOO!" I scream out. I watch as Alpha Ranon and the other wolves begin tearing at Alpha Soran, riping away his flesh and killing him slowly. For what? Because I married him.

I scream out for my husband. I cannot stop screaming as I watch them murder him. My sister is screaming. Alpha Soran is being slaughtered right beside her. His blood is on her.

"Let my sister go!" I cry out to Alpha Ranon.

"Let Candy go," Alpha Ranon says to one of his men. The wolf unties Candy. She runs to me and embraces me.

"We have got to get out of here, Candy," I say to her. I try to stand, and Alpha Ranon's boot hits me in the face. I fall back to the ground.

"Let us go!" Candy screams at Alpha Ranon. He grabs her.

"No, I think I want to keep you as a pet," He says as he holds Candy off the ground. He pulls her close to him and forces a kiss on her lips. He moves her hair and nuzzles in her neck. I can hear him sniffing her.

"Let go of me, you beast," Candy protests. She tries to move, but he is so much larger than her petite frame.

"You smell like a virgin, and I want you—the things I can do to you, Candy. There is no reason to fight it. Just give me what I want, be my little pet," Alpha Ranon says, hissing at my sister.

"Let her go!" I demand, standing to my feet.

"I will let her go after I take what I want from her. You want to watch what I do to your sister?" Alpha Ranon says. He is still holding Candy. He has no intentions of letting either of us go.

Alpha Ranon pulls me to my feet and spins me around on the platform. "Look at all this chaos you caused. They are all dead. It is your fault," Alpha Ranon says.

"This is not my fault!" I scream at him. I try to take Candy from him, but I am no match for him. He grabs me and pulls me into his arms. He is holding both of us. He sniffs me.

"Ummm, you are a virgin too. That shocks me. I figured Alpha Soran tasted you," Alpha Ranon says. He kisses me on the lips.

I push away from him. "Stop it. I am married," I scream at him.

"Your husband is dead, and I plan to mark you as mine. I will let my men have Candy. I would rather have you as my pet," Alpha Ranon says. He drops Candy on the platform.

"Please let her go," I beg him as he carries me with him.

"Do what you want with her sister, then kill her, and burn this place to the ground," Alpha Ranon says to his men. I watch as his men surround my sister. She screams out for me to help her, but I cannot help her.

"NOOOOO!" I scream out.

"Save your strength, Luna. I intend to break you tonight," Alpha Ranon says as he carries me. He walks with me for a while as I listen to the screams of my sister and then fire; there is nothing but fire.

Chapter 3 – The Packhouse of Pain

Kayla POV

Alpha Ranon tormented me right up to the moment we arrived at his pack. I am the only one he took. My parents are dead, my sister and my new husband are both dead. They are all dead! He kept me alive to torture me, and then he will kill me too. First, he wants me to suffer.

Alpha Ranon drags me into the packhouse. Wolves surround me. They are smelling me and touching me. He pushes in front of them. "For now, she is mine, but you will all get a turn with her," He says. I do not know if he is serious or if he is trying to scare me. Either way, I am terrified of what is to come. I am not afraid of death, but the torture before death is what I am most fearful of enduring.

He takes me to a small dog cage that is set on the floor. "Take off all of your clothes and get in there for now," he says. I look down at the cage. I do not even think I will fit inside it.

"No," I say to him and step back from him.

He grabs me and pushes me onto the floor. "Either get into the dog pen like a good bitch, or I will force you in there, and I will break every bone in your body, bitch," Alpha Ranon says.

I sit on the floor and take off my clothes except for my panties, and I crawl into the dog pen and lay on my side. I cannot move the pen is so tiny. "Keep an eye on her," he says to one of the she-wolves in the room.

"Yes, Master," she says, not yes, Alpha, but shesays Master. She is a packhouse pet.

She sits down beside my cage. "If you want water, let me know before he comes back," she says. I nod my head but do not say anything. She moves, grabs a bottle of water that she was sipping on, and hands it to me.

"Thank you," I say to her.

"Drink it fast. Do not ask for water while you are in this pen, trust me. I have been locked in it before, and you do not want water from

Master. Try to stay quiet and behave so he will let you out soon. You do not want to be in this pen long. I have been in it for weeks, and it is horrible," she says.

The wolves do not pay me much attention. They speak to her and touch her when they pass by the dog pen. I am not sure if that is a good thing or a bad thing. Alpha Ranon comes back, and he looks mad as hell. "Did you give her your water?" he asks her.

"Yes, master," she answers. He grabs her and begins shaking her.

"I asked for water," I say, trying to save her, but he does not care. He motions for another wolf to come over to the corner.

"It seems that Shellie needs some discipline, and it would be a good time to show our new pet how we discipline the packhouse pets," Alpha Ranon says to the other wolf.

"Please, master, I am sorry. I will do better," Shellie begs Alpha Ranon. I notice scars on her ankles and her wrists as she moves around, begging for him not to punish her.

"Kayla can take your punishment for you, but you have to go in the dog pen for the rest of the night in her place," Alpha Ranon says.

Kayla looks down at me. Her eyes almost say I am sorry as she nods in agreement to go in the dog pen for the rest of the night. The other wolf opens the door to the dog pen, he pulls me out of the pen fast by my feet, and Shellie goes in the dog pen, taking my place.

The wolf holds me up as a table is brought into the center of the room. Alpha Ranon and the other wolf pin me to the table and then lock my arms and legs in place. I cannot move. Another wolf brings Alpha Ranon a paddle.

"Count to ten," Alpha Ranon says.

"One," I say as he hits me on the paddle. My legs begin to buckle, and he keeps going. When he gets to eight, I can barely stand.

"If you do not stand up, then I will start over, pet," Alpha Ranon says.

"Yes, sir," I say.

He strikes me again hard. "Nine," I say, relieved I have almost made it.

"Do not count that one or this one. I am not your sir. I am your master," he says as he strikes me again.

"Yes, Master," I answer him.

He strikes me two more times, and I finally make it to ten. The wolf unbuckles me from the table, and I fall to the floor. This was supposed to be my wedding night. Instead, I am being tortured and beaten. I know what comes next.

I cannot help but cry as Alpha Ranon pulls me off of the floor. "No tears, my pet, remember this is your wedding night," he says to me.

"Yes, master, " I say to him. I am afraid. I do not want him to hit me again. The wolves are all looking at me and drooling. I look down and realize my panties are gone, and I am completely naked in front of all of them. I want to cry, but he will hurt me more if I do.

I look down at Shellie, and now I understand the marks on her legs and wrists. He beats her a lot. Now there are two of us to beat.

"Take Shellie up to my room, but leave her in the dog pen," Alpha Ranon says to one of his wolves. He pulls me toward another room. I look at the ground as Alpha Ranon takes me through the packhouse. He reaches over and pushes my chin up to make me look at the wolves.

"Look at them. Be proud, my little pet. I am going to mark you as mine tonight," Alpha Ranon says.

Shellie is behind us in the dog pen as we go up the steps to Alpha Ranon's room. The wolf that brought her into the bedroom sets her down on the floor and opens the dog pen for her to get out of it. She crawls out of the pen slowly and comes over to Alpha Ranon. She kneels in front of him and waits for his command.

"Get on your knees with Shellie, my little pet," Alpha Ranon says. I do as he tells me. I look back to see wolves at the door watching the show. They want to see him mark me.

I begin to cry when I see all the wolves watching from the doorway. Alpha Ranon hits me across the face. "Do you want the table again?" he asks.

"No," I answer.

"Then shut up. Remember sweetie, it is your wedding night," Alpha Ranon screams at me.

Chapter 4 – Marry me or die

He tortured her right in front of me. I watched, and so did several wolves as Alpha Ranon took Shellie. He beat her, he raped her, and he made me watch everything he did. He told me I was next, but my turn never came; he kept beating her and taking his anger out on her. I cried as she cried. When she screamed, I screamed.

When Alpha Ranon was finished with her, his men took over. By morning, there is nothing left of Shellie. Her body is cold as it lies here next to me. I am afraid to cry. I am scared to move. He left me alone with her dead body.

I keep reliving the night over and over in my mind. He made me lay in the bed next to them. He would fondle me and taunt me. He spit on me and beat me, but he did not rape me. We watched as his wolves killed her. He wanted it done in front of me so I would comply with his demands. He still wants me to agree to be his mate. I do not understand why?

"I am so sorry. Your life meant something," I say to her. Everyone is dead, and maybe it is my fault.

Alpha Ranon comes back into the bedroom. He throws down a plate of food in front of me. "Eat; you need your strength for tonight," Alpha Ranon says.

I am afraid to ask why I need strength. I grab the food and begin eating it. I get a few bites into my mouth when Alpha Ranon grabs it away from me. "Say thank you, master, or you do not eat," He scolds me.

"Thank you, Master," I say. I smile up at him and try to make him happy. It is hard to smile with a dead body right next to me, but I do the best I can. I want to retreat into my mind or die. I am sure death is coming for me soon enough.

He throws the food down on the floor. "Eat like a dog, little bitch," Alpha Ranon says. I get on the floor and pick up my plate to eat. "NO, like a dog," he says. I do as he says and eat on the floor like the pack dog. That is what I am now anyway. I am his bitch, his pet, his dog.

Wolves come into the room and look at me eating on the floor. One reaches down and pets me on the head. "Such a good little bitch," he says, and then they all laugh.

"Everything is ready for tonight, Alpha," the wolf says. I am listening, but I try not to make it obvious.

The wolves leave. "Come here, Kayla," Alpha Ranon says.

I crawl over to him on all fours, like a good dog. I sit at his feet. "Get up and sit in my lap," he says, patting his knee. I get up and sit on his lap.

"Tonight, you will marry me and be my wife, or you can not marry me tonight and be the packhouse pet. Do you know what it means to be the packhouse pet?" Alpha Ranon asks me. I look over at Shellie.

"I think so, Master," I answer him.

He grabs me tightly. "It means instead of me taking you into our marital bed tonight, you will be tied to the discipline table, and every wolf in this pack will get a turn at you starting with me," Alpha Ranon says.

I look over at Shellie dead. I reach over and touch her. "I understand," I say to Alpha Ranon.

He touches my chin. "Do you want to end up like Shellie?" he asks me. Tears begin to roll down my face.

"No, I do not want to die," I say.

"Then it is settled. We will be married at sunset. My pack will be here, and since you do not have anyone to invite, I have invited other packs to join us. You will be happy and appreciative and say nothing of how you come here," Alpha Ranon says to me.

I nod my head. The back of his hand makes a firm connection to the side of my face. I look up at him. "I am sorry, Master. I will behave and act like a blushing bride tonight," I say. I try to force a smile.

He pulls me up to him and grabs my bare ass. "If you give me any trouble, I will make your first night in my bed hell on earth, little bitch," Alpha Ranon says.

"I understand, Master," I say to him.

He looks down at my breasts and grabs both of them hard. I squeal as he hurts me. My breathing becomes labored. "Maybe I take your virginity now instead of waiting," Alpha Ranon says, throwing me onto the bed. The total weight of his body on me. He is pressed between my legs, and I am at his mercy. I cannot fight him. I look over and see Shellie.

"Master, could you please take care of her first," I asked him. The back of his hand hits my face again.

"Fuck. It looks like the bride will have a black eye on her wedding day," Alpha Ranon says. He gets off of me. He grabs Shellie. He carries her out of the bedroom. I curl up in a ball and begin to cry. I feel a hand touch me. I roll over to see a she-wolf standing by the bed.

"Roll over on your back, little pet," She says. I do as she asks. I do not want to get her in trouble. She secures my legs and wrists with shackles.

"What is this?" I ask.

She does not answer me. She walks out of the bedroom, meeting Alpha Ranon on her way out of the bedroom. The two have a brief exchange, and then he comes back to me. He looks me over, running his hands over my body. He pinches my nipples again until I cry.

"You look perfect, Kayla, and I cannot wait to mark you as mine," Alpha Ranon says. He begins to undress. I look away. I do not even want to look at him.

Chapter 5 – Alpha Maximus

Alpha Maximus POV

I arrive late for my older brother's wedding, very late. My mother is not going to be happy with me at all, but I had business to attend to before I came out here. When I finally make it, all I see is fire for miles, and everything is on fire. As we get closer, there is nothing that is not on fire. I get out of the truck with my security team. The wolves following in another truck rush to my side.

"Find my brother, his new wife, and my parents. Try to put out this fire! NOW!" I order them.

"Yes, Alpha. We will handle it," they say in sync as they start going in different directions to find my parents and put out the fires.

I start walking the grounds, looking for life, but all I see is death. Wolves attacked, murdered. They were attacked on their wedding day. Her pack was a peaceful pack of elders and young women, from what my parents told me; why would anyone want to harm her or my bother and his pack. None of this makes sense. Who would do this? Someone cruelly did this!

"Alpha, we found your parents," Aslin calls to me. I can tell by his voice it is not good. I rush to where Aslin is at. He is kneeled down beside my mother and father. Neither is alive. Both were beaten to death, and I want to know who did this. I let out a mightly growl as my team continues to look for my brother and his wife.

"I will kill whoever is responsible for this," I growl into the night for no one to hear me but the dead and the few wolves with me.

My wolves continue to check each person left lying dead. I was hoping to find someone alive to tell us who did this. A scream is coming from the direction of a platform—a small shout calling for help.

"There is a woman alive over here," Argo call out to me. I rush on the platform where my brother said I do to his new bride and became

Alpha tonight. I look over to see him pulled to pieces. My big brother died on his wedding day, ripped apart.

"Help me," the tiny voice says.

I look down to see the owner of the tiny voice. She is beaten and burned. Her legs are bruised, and she is covered in her own blood. Her dress shredded, and someone took a bite out of her neck. I take her hand, and she begins screaming. "They... They... They too ooo k hhh er," she says. She can barely speak but is trying so hard to help.

"They took her, Kayla the Luna?" I ask her.

She shakes her head. Tears are coming down her face. "Who hurt you and took my brother's wife?" I ask her.

"Car o line is my sis sis sister," she says.

"I will find her, but I need you to tell me who took her?" I ask her again. She takes a deep breath.

"ARrrlllloo," she says.

"Ranon, did you say Ranon as in Alpha Ranon?" I ask her.

"Yessss, he did this," she says slowly.

"We are going to help you. I will take you to a hospital," I say to her. She shakes her head no and cries out in pain.

"I held on," she says, and then she goes limp. I sit down beside her. I growl out into the night again. My wolves join me in growling and howling out in pain.

"We have to take care of the wolves. We cannot leave them like this," I say.

"Yes, sir, we will prepare for them," one of my wolves says. I will take our parents and her parents as well as her sister and my brother back to his pack territory to be buried with honors. I will make sure her pack and my brother's pack receive a funeral before leaving. I cannot believe this happened.

My wolves and I work all night making sure every dead wolf is appropriately buried. We make sure all of the fires are out. My parents and her parents, her sister, and my brother are wrapped in linen and placed in the back of the truck as securely as possible for the journey to my brother's pack territory.

As we drive toward my brother's pack territory, I am at a loss. I should have been there on time to stop all of this. I always travel with a security team, and Aslin and Argo are tough wolves. This would not have happened if I had only done what my mother asked me, and now she is dead, my brother's luna is missing, and fuck, I have to call Marcus.

I take my cell phone out of my pocket and call Marcus. "How is that big wedding?" Marcus asks when he answers the phone.

"Marcus, they are all dead, and his Luna is missing," I say. I do not sugarcoat anything; I just blurt it all out as fast as I can.

"What?" Marcus asks.

"I am taking mom, dad, Soran, and Luna's sister to be buried, and then I am going to find her for Soran," I say.

"Do you know who?" Marcus asks.

I clear my throat. "Alpha Ranon took her," I say.

"Wait, I know where he is. I am sending you his location and anything I can find on him. I am coming. I will let Mindy know what is going on and catch the first flight out," Marcus says.

"See you soon, brother," I say, and then I hang up the phone. I keep thinking about the Luna's sister. She was beaten, raped, and tortured. I cannot even imagine what Alpha Ranon is doing to Luna Kayla to make her submit to him. He will try to break her so he can mark her and take her as his own. Hold out, little wolf, I am coming to save you.

Chapter 6 – His Mark will mean nothing after I kill him

Alpha Maximus POV

I wait for Marcus to come to our brother's wolf land. He takes a late flight leaving his wife and pack behind to help me with burying our brother and parents, as well as our the Luna's sister. I sit on the porch of my brother's house. Now, there is no one here. All of the wolves were at the wedding, and all of his wolves are dead now.

None of this makes sense. From what my parents told me about his bride and her family, they were peaceful people. I left the pack so young that I barely remember Kayla or her family. I do know that her pack was elders and young women. I also know that she chose my brother even though they were not mates. She made a sacrifice to protect her pack. Kayla must be a wonderful wolf, and she does not deserve any of this.

Mother told me that Soran was in love with Kayla and did not care they were not mates. He doted on her and wanted a life with her. Of all wolves, Alpha Ranon wanted her for his. There has to be a reason why he wants her. We are missing something in all of this chaos. Alpha Ranon is known for defeating wolf packs and enslaving other wolves. If he wants Luna Kayla, it is not a coincidence. He has a reason, and I want to know what in the hell it is.

Alpha Ranon is a monster. Now that monster has Kayla. I have to save her and protect it. It is what Soran would want me to do. I will ensure she is taken care of if it is the last thing I do. If the tables were turned, he would protect the woman I loved.

I open another beer and listen to the early, unusual quiet that surrounds me. I look out over my brother's pack land. The land where we grew up, and my father was Alpha. I was happy for him to become Alpha and take my father's place. My call and my brother's call was to the north. We formed our packs and made our parents proud. Soran would have done the same. He would have been a great leader, father, and husband.

Bright lights are coming down the road. I stand and look to see who or what is coming. My security team shift and are waiting for whatever it is. No one should be coming here except Marcus. An SUV pulls into the dirt drive. I throw down the beer bottle. I am ready to take out some of my anger on whoever is in the SUV. My wolves are ready too. This has been a horrible night for everyone.

"Max," Marcus calls out from the SUV.

"Stand down," I call out to my wolves. They turn and go back to what they were doing. I walk over to the SUV.

"I thought you were going to call me when your flight landed so I could send someone for you?" I question Marcus.

He opens the door to the SUV and gets out. "Well, I decided to rent a car to get here. I figured you and your wolves would be upset and maybe drinking. It is fine. I know the way home, Max," Marcus says.

Home, it is hard to remember this place as a childhood home for me. Max and Soran, yes, this is home, but for me, I left the pack when I was twelve to work for Alpha Armed. He trained me to be an Alpha and to take over his pack. He did not have a wife or children. His pack was his life. He chose me out of many wolves to take over his pack. I became his son. I only visited my parents and siblings once a year, but that time was well spent. I have no regrets. I loved both my family with Alpha Armed and my family here.

"I have everything ready. We built a burial structure for all four of them. I do not see a problem allowing the luna's sister to be cremated with Soran and our parents. Unless you have a problem with it?" I inform Marcus of my plans.

Marcus looks to the left of the house and sees the structure built. We will place their bodies on the structure and light it. We will cremate all four of them together, and then they will be at peace. I hope they are at peace. I know if I can rescue Kayla, then Soran will be at peace.

"You and your men did a good thing here. I am sure Kayla will appreciate you taking care of her sister. What are we going to do with the pack land?" Marcus asks me.

I have not thought about it. What will we do with the land we once called home. I look around at the land, and I can almost hear the laughter of the three of us boys running through the grass as children. I smile for a moment, and then I remember that one of us is dead and our parents dead. I quickly become angry.

"Maximus, you can be upset and happy. You do not have to be the macho Alpha all the time. I wish you had someone like Mindy to help you navigate those raw emotions. You know the ones you hide," Marcus says.

I growl loudly into the night. "I do not have time for emotions," I snap at him.

"It seems to me this is emotion, Maximus. You are a great Alpha, but you kind of suck at everything else," Marcus says.

Marcus walks over to the structure. He goes to our mother first. Her voice and scent are forever in my mind. My mother, her beauty, grace, and kindness are gone forever. My father's knowledge, forgiving attitude, and love for his pack are gone forever. The Luna's sister, she fought through the pain to make sure someone knew who had taken her sister; she was brave. Sammy, my brother, dead on his wedding day for loving a woman another Alpha wanted; it is senseless. I will not let them down.

I walk over to the structure after giving Marcus time to say goodbye. I have had plenty of time to say mine tonight. "Are you ready to do this?" I ask him.

"Yes, I am as ready as I will ever be to do this," Marcus says. We each take a torch and begin setting the structure on fire. I feel as if my heart is sinking as I set the structure on fire. I cannot seem weak in front of my brother or my wolves. No matter what anyone says, I have to be strong.

Marcus and I watch in silence as the structure burns. We will bury the ashes in the morning. My wolves howl into the moonlight, giving honor to the fallen, just like we do in battle when we lose a wolf. This was not a fair fight. This was an ambush. There will be no honor in his death or honorable burial when I kill Alpha Ranon. I will put his head on a stake and mount it to the entrance of his pack territory. He will regret touching my family.

"We should give it to her," I say.

Marcus looks at me, confused. "What?" he asks me.

"The pack land, we should gift it to Kayla. She deserves it. She will need a home and a place to build a life. I will help her build a pack and make sure she is safe," I say.

Marcus looks back to the burning fire. I hear our laughter again. It is almost a haunting sound from our childhood. "I agree, but first we have to get her back from Ranon before he kills her too," Marcus says.

"He is not going to kill her. He wants her," I say.

"What if he marks her as his?" Marcus asks me.

"His mark will mean nothing after I kill him," I answer.

Chapter 7 – Are you Ready

Luna Kayla POV

"Are you ready, Kayla?" Alpha Ranon asks me.

I do not answer him. I look away and stare at the wall. I can feel the weight of him on the bed. He pushes my legs apart, and then his fingers invade me. He slides them in and out of me hard. "Looks like you are ready for me, Kayla," Alpha Ranon says. I still say nothing. I keep looking at the way.

He grabs my face. "Look at your master," Alpha Ranon says.

"Yes, Master," I say to him. I look at him as he slides his fingers in and out of me.

"Tell me that you want me," Alpha Ranon demands. I look away. He shoves his fingers into me hard. I scream out from the pain as he pushes three fingers into me and keeps pushing up. PAIN PAIN I feel nothing but Pain.

"Tell me you want me, or I can make this much worse," Alpha Ranon says.

I must comply. I am in so much pain as he pushes inside me. "I want you, Master," I say to him. He smiles at me.

"Look at me when I play with your pussy," Alpha Ranon says.

I look at him. I want to look away, but he makes it hurt worse every time I do. He pulls his fingers out of me. "Now, I am going to make you mine permanently, Kayla. You will be mine forever, my whore, my pet, my wife," Alpha Ranon says. He pushes my legs apart and forces himself inside me.

Pain, all I feel is pain. My heart is breaking. All I can think about is Soran and how much he loved me. Now, he is dead. Maybe I should have saved all of us the pain and taken Alpha Ranon as my husband instead of Soran. Now, my sweet Soran is dead, and I am trapped in the packhouse. I am being forced to marry Alpha Ranon anyway. I have two choices; one marry the wolf I hate, or two, I will be trapped in the packhouse as a pet.

I stare at the wall as Alpha Ranon takes my virginity from me. I try not to cry, but the pain is too much. I am bound by the silver shackles, forced into place and forced into obedience. I could not fight him off if I wanted to fight him. He wants to defeat me. I feel defeated as he bites me and takes me hard. He wants me to feel nothing but pain.

As the pain of his invasion pulsates through my body, and he sweats on me, pushing into me hard and trying to hurt me, all I can think about is how sweet Soran was, how choosing him was the right thing to do and how I wanted to be a mother to his children. Alpha Ranon breaks my concentration and kisses me. His tongue invades my mouth. I move my head to the side to try to escape his kiss. He bites my neck and howls as he forcefully takes me hard.

"You are mine, Kayla, mine minemine," Alpha Ranon moans and growls as he forces himself in and out of me. My virginity is gone at the hands of this ruthless wolf. I saved myself for marriage, and it is gone. I am ruined now. Who would want a stained, broken wolf even if I did escape? I will be branded a whore.

I cry. I did not want him to see me cry, but I cannot stop crying. I want to go home. I want my husband and my family back. I close my eyes and try to think of my family. A sharp pain hits my face and forces me to open my eyes.

"Stop crying bitch and tell me how good it feels to be with a real wolf," Alpha Ranon says as he slaps me across the face. I refuse to say anything. He drives into me harder.

"I can make this the worst day of your life," Alpha Ranon says. I know he is not bluffing. I can only imagine how much he could hurt me.

He pumps into me harder. "No one will want you now. You will always smell like me. Every wolf that comes near you will know I took you first. You are mine forever, Kayla," Alpha Ranon growls at me.

"NOOOO!" I scream as loud as I can. I have had enough, and I will not be compliant anymore. I try to move, sending waves of pain through my flesh as the silver burns my skin.

"Soran!" I scream for my husband. I want him to rescue me. I want him to come for me, but it will not happen. Soran is dead, and it is all my fault. I deserve all of this.

My screams and begging only ignite a flame inside Alpha Ranon. He laughs and takes me harder. He leans into my face, trapping me forcing me to look at him. He buries his tongues in my mouth. His hand is on my throat as he kisses me. "Kiss me whore," Alpha Ranon says to me.

The sounds of the bed banging against the wall and our skin making contact echo through the room. I can hear wolves howling and taunting me as Alpha Ranon shows his dominance over me. I can either be his whore or everyone's whore.

"You are mine, Kayla, SAY IT! Tell me that you belong to me!" Alpha Ranon demands.

His hand on my throat, demanding I submit to him. "I am yours, Master," I say. I want to rebel, but how can I? I have to find a way to fight, but maybe the best thing is to be compliant right now.

Alpha Ranon finally begins to groan loudly and pushes into me, spilling himself into me. He gets off of me and sits on the bed beside me. I am just thankful it is over and that he is done with me. He looks back at me. "I was easy on you now. I need you to walk when you say I do to serve me forever. But tonight, after you become mine, I will break you, Kayla. I will break you!" Alpha Ranon says.

One of the wolves comes into the bedroom with the pet that shackled me to the bed earlier. "We want to help you break her," the wolf says.

Alpha Ranon looks at me. "Well, maybe one more round before we get ready for our wedding," Alpha Ranon says.

"NO, NO, NO!" I scream. I cannot take it again! I cry as the three of them surround me. Someone please help me!

Chapter 8 – I am a prisoner

Luna Kayla POV

They toy with me, play with me, and treat me like I am nothing. The pain the three of them put me through is unbearable. I cannot help but scream as they each take a turn hurting me. Alpha Ranon and his wolf, Pierce, are determined to break me, and the she-wolf is willing to help them. How could she help them hurt me? She is a hostage just like me and probably just trying to survive.

Alpha Ranon takes me again, and Pierce is beneath me, taking my back hole. The she-wolf beats me as I scream out for help. "Soran!" I scream out for my dead husband. The three of them laugh. The more I cry, the more they enjoy hurting me. Before long, more wolves are coming to watch as the three of them torture me. Finally, it is over. Alpha Ranon, Pierce, and the she-wolf leave me screaming and crying.

I lay in pain and crying, alone and defeated. I scream out, growl, and cry. I can hear the laughter coming from the wolves and Alpha Ranon. I have a decision to make. Do I let him break me, fall in line, and suffer through this for the rest of my life, or do I fight back? How do I fight back when there are so many against me? How can I live like this? I cannot live like this.

The door opens slowly. My stomach clinches, thinking Alpha Ranon is coming back to take me again or Pierce is coming to take me from underneath again. I am in so much pain, and I scream as the door opens, only to be hit with the laugher and taunts of the wolves. Everything hurts. Every place they forced themselves into hurts. Alpha Ranon and his wolf took everything from me; there is nowhere on my body that has not been assaulted by Alpha Ranon and his wolf now. No part of my body is still a virgin.

"Shhh. It would be best if you calmed down," the she-wolf says as she comes into the bedroom with me. I look at her with disgust. She was a part of the last break Kayla session and seemed to enjoy the things she did to me.

"What do you want?" I ask her. I try to move. I would love to get my hands on her, but then what? Is any of this really her fault. Maybe not, but did she have to enjoy it so much?

She comes to me, moves my hair from my face, and looks me over. "I am here to clean you up and help you get ready for your wedding. It is a big night for you, Kayla," she says. I look into her eyes, looking for any sign of feelings behind her eyes. She seems cold and distant. I am sure whatever feelings she had, they beat it out of her.

"Here is what is going to happen, and it is important that you do exactly as I say, or we both will end up tied to a discipline table getting a beating and probably worse. Can you listen to me and comply?" she asks me.

"I will not cause you any trouble, " I say to her.

"I am going to unshackle you from the bed and help you out of the bed. We will go into the bathroom where I will shower you and then dress you for the wedding. I will stay with you until it is time for you to go to the altar and marry Alpha Ranon," she says.

"I promise not to run or cause you any problems," I say.

The she-wolf unshackles me and helps me to sit on the side of the bed. The pain between my legs and coming from my bottom is unreal as I sit on the side of the bed, and I want to scream, but I will not give them the pleasure of my screams anymore. She grabs my face. "Do not think that I will not kick your ass myself if you run. I will not end up like Shellie because of you. It is your fault they killed her," she says.

I nod my head. I know she will not help me. She is just trying to survive, and I understand that. She wants to live, and I will not cause her any more pain. I damn sure do not want her to end up like Shellie.

My legs buckle as I stand up to follow her to the bathroom. She looks at me coldly. "You will not make it a month," she says. She is probably right. If I am not going to make it anyway, then maybe I should fight back, but not now, not when I can cause her pain or anyone else. When I make my move, it needs to be on me.

I walk out of the bedroom with my head high. The wolves surround me, growling and taunting me. "Ummmm, you smell like a whore," one of them says. "I hope she does not make it to the altar. Maybe we can all have a turn," another wolf says.

One wolf grabs my naked body. He kisses me behind the ear and pins me to the wall. "Alpha said we can all have a turn at that ass," he says. He grinds against me. I pull away from him, and I am quickly slapped to the ground.

I hear a growl coming from the front of the house. "Let her be, as long as she falls in line and is mine, then hands-off," Alpha Ranon says. He pushes his way through the wolves.

"Now, Kayla, do you want to be mine or the packhouse pet?" Alpha Ranon asks me to make sure I have made up my mind. I look at the wolves wanting me. I will be dead by nightfall.

I look at Alpha Ranon. "I already told you that I am yours, Master," I answer him. I have to get out of this packhouse and away from all these wolves. It is the only way I will ever be able to run.

The wolf growls toward me. "Not fair, Alpha, you let Pierce have a turn with her," he protests.

"True, but Pierce was only trying to help break her, and he did as I told him. I do not think you would comply, and I do not want you to mark my bride," Alpha Ranon answers.

I follow the she-wolf to the bathroom, thankful that Alpha Ranon did not allow that wolf to have any part of me. I get into the shower, and the she-wolf begins helping me shower. Everything is hurting, and she is so rough with me.

"I do not want you to stink when you get married," she says.

"Why me?" I ask.

She looks at me. She slaps me on the face and grabs me by the throat. "Do you not get it, you stupid bitch! He wants you. Not me, you! I hope he changes his mind and lets all of the wolves have you until you die," she screams at me.

The bathroom door comes open, and Alpha Ranon comes into the bathroom. He reaches into the shower and pulls her off of me. He takes her out of the bathroom, and I hear him growling at her. "Pierce, come get your bitch and handle her," Alpha Ranon screams.

Moments later, he comes into the bathroom. I am still showering. "I will have another she-wolf come help you get ready for the wedding. Try to behave yourself and make tonight go well for both of us. If you comply and act right, then I will move you out of the packhouse," Alpha Ranon says.

Good then, I can run the first chance I get. I stand in the shower, letting the water run over my body. I just have to hold on and gain his trust, and then I can get out of here. I can do this. I can maintain.

The door opens, and I see the wolf from earlier. He is standing outside the shower and licking his lips. "Now that the Alpha is gone, I can fuck you, little bitch," he says. He reaches into the shower and grabs me. He throws me onto the floor of the bathroom.

I scream out for help. No one is coming. He holds me with one hand and unzips his pants with the other. I can feel him at my entrance. I close my eyes, and then someone pulls him off of me. I open my eyes to see her. She throws him out of the bathroom and locks the door.

"Greg is such a dick," she says.

"Thank you," I say as she helps me off the floor. She looks at the bruises on me. She shakes her head.

"I am sorry that my brother is an asshole. I am sorry this is happening to you. I cannot help you, but I can protect you from the other wolves. The best thing you can do is marry Ranon and please him. Your life will be easier if you do. I am Julie, Alpha Ranon's sister. I am a prisoner here too," she says. She pulls me into her arms and holds me. I cry into her shoulder and let everything out.

Chapter 9 – I will honor my brother above everything

Maximus POV

It is not much for me to do except worry and wait while Marcus handles the time and location for the destruction of Alpha Ranon. Marcus knows where Alpha Ranon is located, but we cannot exactly just walk into his pack, grab Kayla and leave with a commotion. The minute we grab Kayla, all hell will break loose, and I am ready to fight for her. Marcus insists we need a plan, and Marcus is the better wolf to make the plan. I want to walk into Alpha Ranon's house, behead him and chuck him to his wolves. I want to see him hurt, and in my anger, I could risk the life of Luna Kayla. That would not be what my brother would want. Soran would want my ultimate goal to be to save Luna Kayla. I will honor My brother above everything.

"Max," Marcus calls out to me. I get up from the porch step. I finish my beer and follow my brother into the house. It is so eery being here. I know Marcus does not feel that way, but to me, there are too many ghosts in this house, and I hate being here. That is why I suggested we give this land to Kayla. Marcus and Mindy have a home. I do not want to be here. Kayla has no one and nowhere to call home. I will help her build this place to its former bubbling wolf population, but first, we have to get her here.

"Yeah, did you figure out how to get Kayla away from that monster?" I ask Marcus. He knows what I want to do, and I can see it all over his face, a plan to try to keep me from killing an entire wolf pack. I want to avenge my brother, but Kayla is the priority first. Her safety and then my revenge.

"Max, there is a celebration tonight, and we are invited," Marcus says.

"He is celebrating killing our brother, and he invited us to come!" I growl. Marcus steps back. He is smaller than me. When I am angry, I tower over my younger brother.

"He plans to marry Kayla and take her as his mate," Marcus says.

I begin pacing back and forth. I growl, I punch the wall, and finally, I stop. I take a deep breath and look at my younger brother, who is trying to remain calm in this situation. I have never understood how Marcus and Soran could always remain calm. Not me, I am the hot head, the kill them all and sort it out later wolf. I take after our mother. Although mother was one of the kindest wolves you would ever meet, she also, like me, had one hell of a temper. I guess that is why we always clashed over the years. "What are we going to do, Marcus? What is your plan to get our brother's wife to safety?" I growl.

My brother pauses and gives me a moment to just be angry, then he steps up to me. "Max, please let me explain everything, and then you can be angry or protest or whatever you need to do so we can get this show on the road. We do not have a lot of time," Marcus says.

"Okay, Marcus. Lay it all out for me," I say to him.

I take a seat at the kitchen table. I hate being here more and more. I hear my mother and father's voice speaking to me as I sit here waiting for Marcus to lay out his plan. I can hear Soran laughing and joking as he always did. Marcus has always been the level-headed one. This place is an emotional train wreck for me.

"Ranon plans to marry Kayla tonight. He is trying to hurry things along to get us off him. Thankfully we have a little help on the inside. A wolf reached out to Mindy and told her everything. She is trying to protect Kayla, but she said things are bad for Kayla and that Ranon has already hurt her pretty badly," Marcus says.

I know what he means. He means that Alpha Ranon has raped her and probably beaten her. "How bad?" I ask.

I am not sure I want the answer. "The wolf that is helping us wants out too. She is Alpha Ranon's sister, and she desperately wants away from him. She told Mindy he would kill her for her betrayal. She said she cannot watch what he is doing anymore," Marcus says.

I slam my fist into the table. "HOW BAD HAS HE HURT HER!" I growl.

"I do not know. She only said it was bad and that we needed to get her out of there. Kayla is not completely compliant with him. She is fighting at times and compliant at times. If she fights him, he could kill her," Marcus says.

"He will kill her, but first, he will try to break her," I say.

I can feel the well of anger forming in me, and I want to explode. I want to go straight to this wedding and rip Alpha Ranon's head off. I begin breathing hard just thinking about what he is doing to her and how much he has hurt her. I have to save her for my brother.

"I have a plan. We can get her before the ceremony, but we need to hurry, and I need you to remain calm. If things go sideways, then by all means kill them all, but if we can just get Luna Kayla and the wolf protecting her out, then let's do it without losing any more life tonight," Marcus says.

"What about the next she-wolf he kidnaps? Should he not pay for this atrocity with his life?" I ask.

Marcus knows I am right. If we let Alpha Ranon live, his reign of terror will continue. "Fine new plan, get her out and her protector safely, then kill them all. Are you happy now?" Marcus asks me.

I stand up from the table, towering over Marcus again. "I will be happy when he is dead, and she is safe," I say

Chapter 10 -Survival

Luna Kayla POV

Julie dresses me in a white gown and a white veil. She does my hair and my makeup. I look in the mirror at myself when she finishes painting me to cover the bruises on my face and neck. "I think you did a good job," I say to her. I want to scream and run from this place, but Alpha Ranon would kill her if I ran. He would blame her and kill us both.

"I am sorry for all of this. Just try to be compliant. Please, Kayla, I beg you to try to make him happy," Julie begs me. She is crying as she pleads with me. I wonder did he threaten her or does she really feel for me. How can her own brother treat her this way?

The packhouse is practically empty right now. Only a few wolves and she-wolves remain behind with Julie and me. It is strange the packhouse is not echoing the growls and taunts of the other wolves. It is peaceful for the first time since Alpha Ranon brought me here against my will.

"He will not bring you back here tonight. He will take you to his home. Be good to him, do what he says, and you can survive the night. You do not want to be brought back here and handed over to the wolves as a gift. That is exactly what he will do if you disobey him. He will go out and kidnap another wolf to be his bride. It will be easier on you away from the packhouse. You do not want to be a packhouse pet," Julie says. I shake my head to let her know I understand. I do wonder how many there have been before me. Why did he want me so bad that he killed my husband, our family, and our packs? Was it my rejection? Did that push him over the edge?

In my mind, all I can think about is running. I am in so much pain that I know I will not get far if I run. With all of them chasing me, I would be dead before I got to the treeline. If I did live the torture, beatings, and being raped by all of them, that would kill me or make me wish I was dead. Maybe Julie is right, and I should comply with him, smile, and try to survive for now.

The door opens, and a tall wolf comes into the room, where Julie tries to calm me and prep me for my night with Alpha Ranon. Not sure it could be worse than what he has already done to me, but Julie seems to want to help me. "We are ready for the blushing bride," the wolf says. He reaches over and touches my breast.

"Leave her alone; she belongs to your Alpha," Julie snaps at him.

"She will not make it as his. I bet she will be a packhouse pet by the end of the week. I plan to get to the front of the line. I want to make her scream," the wolf says, reaching into my dress. I back away from him and scream as loud as I can.

My scream distracts the wolf and gives Julie time to punch him in the face. He backs away from her. "Get out, or I will tell my brother you touched me. I know that will not go over well with my brother," Julie threatens the wolf.

"Bring the bitch out. The guests are here, and we are ready to get this over with so we can start the real party," the wolf laughs. I wonder what the real party is and if it has anything to do with me.

Julie hugs me, and the two of us walk from the room and toward the front of the house. Julie seems distracted as she helps me out the door. My legs begin to buckle as we make our way toward Alpha Ranon. I cannot help but start to cry as Julie lets go of my hand and I walk toward Alpha Ranon alone. When I reach Alpha Ranon, he leans over and grabs me around the waist hard. "Stop your fucking crying, or else I will beat you so badly tonight that no one will even recognize you," he whispers into my ear.

"Sorry," I say to him.

I look over and notice a table beside us. It is a table with shackles, just like the discipline table. "What is that?" I ask him.

"For the party after the wedding," he says. He smiles at me, a devilish smile. I begin to cry. I cannot stop. I can feel my heart beating into my chest. I scream out.

"PLEASE, SOMEONE HELP ME!" I scream as loud as I can. No one moves. No one cares.

"Get that bitch!" Alpha Ranon growls.

I turn and begin to run toward the treeline. Please let me make it away from here. I can hear Alpha Ranon's wolves howling, growling, and taunting me as the wolves run toward me. I can listen to their calls and fighting over who will get me first. They will kill me, but not if I get away. I feel someone beside me as I hit the treeline.

Julie is running with me. "Shift and run; I will try to fight them off," she says. I shift into my wolf and run, but I am hurting. My legs are weak. I am weak. My wolf cannot heal me, and I will not make it. I see someone ahead of me. A group of them made it ahead of me. No, that is not Alpha Ranon's wolves. It is someone else. Someone that can help me get away from here.

One of the wolves grabs me, and I fall into his arms. I am tired and hurting. "Little wolf," he says so kindly.

"Please do not hurt me," I cry.

He wraps me in his embrace, and I fall into darkness. "She passed out," a male wolf voice says. I hear others talking and then a commotion. I cannot open my eyes. I am falling into the darkness farther and farther. The darkness feels like a warm blanket. I do not fight it. I need to heal.

Chapter 11 - Recovery

Alpha Maximus

She rests in the bedroom that once belonged to my parents. She sleeps, and I keep watch over her. I cannot take my eyes off of her. I want to make sure she is okay but not invade her privacy. She has a long road ahead of her from her looks, and I plan to honor my brother by being with her every step of the way. She will not be alone in this. She will need a lot, and I will make damn sure she gets everything she needs, no matter what it is or how hard it is to get.

"How is she?" Marcus asks me. He is behind me as I peer into the bedroom. I know Marcus wants to get home to Mindy and needs to wrap this up as soon as possible. He can go home. It is fine with me. I do not need him for this part. He will just be in the way.

"She is weak. I am worried about her. The healer has been with her a few times this morning, but she refuses to wake up. He said her wolf is in shock and trying to heal her body," I say.

Marcus takes a deep breath and then places his hand on my shoulder. "Jules, the Alpha's sister, is being taken to another pack to hide. She has asylum with the Crescents, and they will take care of her for now until she can figure out what to do. Now we have to figure out what to do with Kayla," Marcus says.

"I will figure it out," I snap at him. I do not even want his help now.

Although I am thankful that Jules helped us, I am not concerned for her well-being, only for Kayla. I have to make things right for her. She begins groaning. I open the door, and she reaches above her; she screams and then falls back to sleep.

"She is really shaken up, isn't she?" Marcus says.

I look at him and shake my head. Sometimes, it blows my mind when I talk to him about how far away from real emotions he is to be a family man. What did he think she would be like?

"Marcus, what the hell do you think he was doing with her? How did you expect her to act once we rescued her?" I ask him. I know Marcus is my brother, but sometimes I think there is something wrong with him.

"I know, but I did not expect her to be so broken," Marcus says.

I look down at her, sleeping and trying to heal. "She is not broken; she is strong. She survived, she ran, and she will heal! I will make sure of that," I say.

"I can take her home with me. Mindy can look after her," Marcus suggests. Yeah, Mindy, sure. Mindy is an excellent Luna, but it is not going to happen unless it involves her nails and hair. I do not see Mindy making sure Kayla is cared for, fed, bathed, and healing.

"I am staying here with her. I have already told you what I plan to do with this place. I will help her, and she will have a home," I say.

"What if she does not want this place? And what about your pack?" Marcus asks.

I stand over my brother, towering over him. "I have already made arrangements for my pack. I am not leaving her. Go home to your wife and let me handle this, brother," I say to Marcus. He backs down. That is right, little brother, back the fuck down. I am about to lose it on you.

Marcus walks toward the bedroom door. "You could at least ask her what she wants before you start making decisions for her," Marcus says.

"She is the Luna of this pack, and the land is hers!" I remind Marcus.

Marcus steps to me. "What pack? They are all dead except the few wolves that were here instead of at the wedding!" Marcus yells at me.

I turn away from Marcus. I would hate for Luna Kayla to wake up to me choking the life out of Marcus. "Goodbye, Brother," I say to him as I look out the window. I am done talking to him.

Marcus leaves, and I do not leave Kayla to say goodbye. I already said my goodbye to him. She has not woken up entirely yet. She screams for Soran, cries, and moves her arms around as if she is fighting off someone. I am afraid to leave her alone. I do not want her to wake up, and no one be here with her. She needs me, and I will help her, for Soran, to honor him.

"SORAN!" she screams out louder than before. I rush to her, and I take her hand. She squeezes my hand. "I knew you would save me," she says. Tears are flowing down her face. She begins to open her eyes. She looks at me.

"Luna Kayla, I am Maximus. I am Soran's brother," I say softly. She looks at me as if she is trying to focus.

"Where am I?" she asks me. She blinks rapidly and tries to move. She looks around the room.

"You are home. I brought you to the home of my parents. You and Soran would have lived here after the wedding, so I brought you here to heal," I say to her. She looks around, confused.

"Soran? My pack? My sister? My parents?" she asks, and then her face turns to horror as she remembers.

She lays back in the bed. "Please do not let him take me. I cannot take anymore," Luna Kayla screams out.

She squeezes my hand. "I promise to keep you safe, little wolf," I say to her.

She closes her eyes. For a moment, she looks peaceful, and then she sits up in the bed. "SORAN!" she screams for him.

I take her into my arms and hold her. "Please do not beat me again. I will behave," Kayla cries. I want to take her pain from her.

"No one will ever hurt you again, little wolf," I whisper into her ear. I hold her frail body in my arms. Her body is covered in so many bruises and lashes it makes me and my wolf angry. How could someone hurt such a beautiful, sweet young woman?

She pulls away from me and looks into my eyes. "Help me," she says, her eyes pleading for help.

"You are safe," I tell her again. She looks around the room and is searching for him. She is scared, and nothing I can say will reassure her she is safe yet.

She lays back in the bed and falls back into a deep sleep, still holding my hand. I brush the hair from her face and notice more bruises on her. There is no part of her that Ranon left untouched.

Chapter 12 – Tormented Souls

Alpha Max

I leave her only for a moment. I need to step away from her cries. The torment in her soul, it pains me in a certain way that it should not. I cannot bear seeing her lying there in pain and crying out for my brother, but I have to do this for Kayla, my brother, and his pack. I have to be loyal to her.

One of the few wolves left here, an Omega named Char, goes into the bedroom to sit with her to give me a break. I need just a few moments to pull myself together. I need to regroup so I can be one hundred percent for her when she wakes up and wants answers. I know she was there, and I know she saw everything that happened, but the burning question is, how much does she remember? The other question is, how will I have the courage to tell her everything that she does not remember?

I take a deep breath and walk out onto the porch. I settle into a chair and look out over the vast land, surrounded by beautiful woods. I remember shifting for the first time on this porch and running as fast as possible to those woods. My father ran behind me, and we ran for miles. It is one of the few times he and I shared a moment, and then, not too long after that, I left and took my place with my pack. I have no regrets. I know I did not belong here. I never fit in with my family or my brothers. I was different. Who am I kidding? I am still different from Marcus. I will never be like them, not that it matters now.

"Alpha Maximus, she is awake and crying," Char screams as she comes through the front door.

I leap to my feet and follow her back to the bedroom. When I step into the bedroom, Kayla is screaming and crying. She is trying to move her body. She sees me and screams a blood curling scream. "HELP!" She screams out.

I go to her and kneel beside her bed. "I am not here to hurt you. I brought you here. Do you remember anything?" I ask her.

Her breathing is all over the place. "I ... I cannot remember. Wait, Candy? Soran? Where is my mother? Where am I?" she says as she is looking around, questioning her own sanity.

I take her hand and motion for Char to come closer. "This is Char. She is one of the only wolves left of Soran's pack. I am Alpha Maximus. I am Soran's brother," I say to her. There is so much more to tell her, but I think it is better to give her a little information at a time and not bombard her with everything that happened at once. I have a feeling the floodgates will open soon enough, and she will remember everything.

She holds the blanket against her body tightly. Char bathed her and put some clothes on her, but I am sure she is wondering many things, including who's clothes she is wearing.

Her eyes seem to be moving a million different ways. "I am not in my room," she says.

"No, this was my parent's room and the house, and this room belongs to you now," I say.

"To Soran and me, I know, but I do not remember coming here," Kayla says.

She looks down at her arms her wrist, and she begins inspecting her body. "What is the last thing you remember?" I ask her.

A lightbulb seems to go off over her head, and she screams out. "SORAN!" she screams. She begins to make a bubbling sound and sobbing. I take her into my arms, and she screams louder. I hold her against my better judgment until she finally settles down and lays her head into me.

"He killed my Soran," she whispers. She keeps repeating his name.

"I am so sorry, Kayla," I say to her as I continue to hold her.

I motion for Char to leave us, there is much more for us to talk about, and we should probably do it in private. I had not planned to go into any details today, but since she is awake and trying to remember, maybe I should.

"He wanted me to choose between Soran and my sister, but Soran told him to let Candy live. He gave his life for hers, but it was a lie! He killed her," Kayla continues. Her heart is breaking, and so is mine as she relives all of the horrible things that happened on her wedding day.

"I brought your sister here and buried her," I tell her. She pulls away from me. She looks into my eyes.

"Thank you for that. Soran is here?" she asks.

"Yes. We cremated my parents, Soran, and your sister together. I gathered the ashes, and they are buried here on your land," I say to her.

"Will you show me where?" Kayla asks.

"I will show you when you are better. I am staying here with you until you are on your feet and we have everything running smoothly here for you," I say.

"What do you mean?" Kayla asks me.

"The pack land is yours. My brother, Marcus, and I want to make sure you have a place that is yours. Soran would want you to have it. I know he loved you," I say.

Kayla lays back down and sinks into the pillow. "I want to rest now if that is okay?" she asks as if I would say no to her. She needs to rest, and she needs to recover.

"I will be on the front porch. Char is in the kitchen cooking. If you need anything, we will be close by for you," I say to her.

She nods her head. I walk out of the door and start to close it. I hear her begin to cry as I go out of the room. Maybe she needs to cry alone instead of with someone on top of her. Perhaps she needs to grieve her husband, and she may just need to grieve the fact Ranon tortured her.

Char is in the kitchen, cooking as I make my way back to the front porch to give her quiet or give myself quiet. I am not sure what I need right now, but I have to find the strength to be here for her.

I sit outside for over an hour. I can smell the food Char is cooking, and I think maybe I should eat something. I get out of my chair, and Kayla is standing at the door. She is wearing a long white gown that Char brought over for Kayla.

She comes through the door to the porch and joins me. "I have been watching you for a few minutes. I did not want to disturb you," Kayla says.

"I want you to disturb me. I am here for you," I tell her. I reach for her hand and lead her into a chair next to mine. I sit back down next to her.

"Are you okay?" I ask her.

Tears begin forming in her eyes. "I am not sure. I remember everything. I remember the screams of my family and how Soran died. Ranon butchered him, and he let his wolves rape my sister. Why?" Kayla questions.

"I do not know why he did what he did, but he did pay for it," I say. I know killing Alpha Ranon is not a comfort after what Kayla has been through, but maybe it will help her heal somewhat.

"Now, here I am with what ten wolves and a pack to run, with no husband and no family. I am crushed. I have no idea what I am supposed to do now. I am lost, Alpha Max," Kayla says.

I take her hand. "I will stay as long as you need me," I say.

I look into her eyes as I hold her hand. When my wolf decides to get involved, I am only trying to comfort her and give her some peace. I can feel my wolf howling as I look into her eyes. Fuck, this cannot be happening to me now. I am here to help her, not ... NO! NO! NO! My wolf is screaming for her. MATE!

"Mate," she whispers.

Chapter 13 – Why does he care

Kayla POV

He leaves me to rest and to sort through all the thoughts running through my mind. I still hurt from everything Ranon did to me. I do not want to talk about that, not now or ever. I want to bury the things Ranon did to me and let all the feelings and memories rot somewhere. I cannot face any of that now.

He is kind to me, even though he does not have to be kind or helpful or even be here. He could have handed everything over to me and left, but he stays to help me and make sure I could handle it. Maybe he is worried about me taking over his family's land. No, that is not it. Soran told me once about Alpha Maximus and how he left as a child. He said he never fit in with the family. It must be hard for him to be here.

I scoot to the side of the bed. I gather my strength, and after a few failed attempts, I finally can get to my feet. I walk carefully to the door and then make my way into the kitchen, where Char is finishing up the meal. "Luna, do you need help?" she asks me.

It is odd to hear the word Luna, and someone is talking about me. Luna, I guess I am the Luna of this pack; what is left of it anyway. If there are only five wolves left in the pack, I will serve this pack; that is what Soran would want of me. At least, I think that is what he would wish for me to do. I really have no idea what Soran would want from me.

Soran and I were not mates. He was kind, he cared for me, and I cared for him, but we were not chosen mates; we were arranged. What if I never find my mate? I think I would be okay with that. I do not believe there is any way I will ever marry again, no matter if my mate jumps in front of me, takes my hand, and begs for me. I honestly never want a man to touch me again. My only encounter with a man sexually is a nightmare I never want to relive, and no man will understand that pain or any of the things I have been through when I decided to marry. My focus should be on Soran's pack, and that will be my main concern.

I watch Alpha Maximus as he sits on the front porch. He seems occupied, and maybe it is the worry; perhaps he needs to get back to his wolves. Being here with me cannot be easy for him. I hate to be a burden to anyone. I am not sure if he is waiting for me to tell him how Soran died or if he is really here to help me. I have no idea of his intentions. He stands up, and I look at him. He seems shocked as he peers through the door at me.

I realize I am standing in the doorway in a long white gown. I must look frightful. He opens the door and invites me onto the porch with his beautiful eyes.

"I am sorry, Alpha. I did not mean to disturb you," I say to him. He smiles at me, and it is so beautiful. It feels wonderful to see such a beautiful sight, especially right now when I feel as if my body is coming apart.

"It is okay. I want you to disturb me," Alpha Max says. His words radiate through me. I am not sure why, but I start telling him how Soran died and how he sacrificed himself to save Candy, not that it did any good. Ranon still killed her.

Alpha Max listens to me, and I feel as if I can tell him anything. He reaches over and takes my hand. "I will stay as long as you need me," he says. I look into his beautiful eyes, and like a ton of bricks, it hits me. He cannot be. This is too soon. How can this happen right now?

"Mate," I whisper so quietly.

Alpha Maximus lets go of my hand and stand up. He moves off the porch quickly. I know this is not something he wants, and I do not want it either. "I will not be the type of wolf that takes his brother's wife," Alpha Max says. He turns back and looks at me.

"I have no intentions of taking a mate or ever having a man in my bed," I say to him sternly.

"Good, then there is no need to discuss this any further, correct?" Alpha Max asks me as if I am a child needing to be corrected. This infuriates me.

"I am not a child. I am a grown woman, Alpha Max, and I will not be talked down to, got it?" I bark at him.

Alpha Max shakes his head. "I meant no disrespect to you, Luna Kayla. I am a single wolf, and I like it that way, okay. You just lost your husband, my brother, and have been through an ordeal, so we both agree that for now, we need to only concentrate on the pack and, most importantly, your recovery," Alpha Maximus says.

"I agree, but I hope that you will stay. I want you to stay as you promised," I say. I have no idea how to handle a pack or a pack's needs.

"I will keep my word to you, Luna Kayla. I will help you and show you how to run a pack. I will help you build this pack up, and maybe someday you will return it to its former glory, only better," Alpha Maximus says.

"Thank you," I say to him.

I look over to see Char standing at the door like she just walked in on a private conversation and is unsure if she should speak up or not. "Dinner is ready," Char says.

Alpha Maximus and I go into the house. We sit down and eat together. We are careful not to touch one another and try to avoid eye contact, but my wolf is going insane. My wolf wants to feel his touch and look into his eyes. I am not sure I will ever be ready for someone to touch me again.

I look up from my plate and catch a glimpse of him. Our eyes lock, and I melt. Every part of me melts for him. This cannot be happening to me. I cannot stand the thought of a man touching my body or being inside me, but Alpha Maximus is doing something to me. Mate! My wolf screams for him. I can feel the tears coming again.

"I am sorry," I say as I spring from the table. I rush back to the bedroom. I close the door and go straight to the bed. I fall into the bed and close my eyes. I hold the pillow close to my face, and I scream as loud as I can into the pillow. What kind of sick joke is this?

Chapter 14 – You can give me peace

No one bothers me through the evening after dinner, and I do not leave my room. I go to the window and look out over the massive land illuminated by the moonlight. I cannot believe this would have been the home of my Alpha and me, not it is only my home. I understand why Alpha Maximus and his brother chose to walk away and allow me to have the land and the pack. I am, no, I was married to his brother, and technically I am the Luna of this pack and should be here, but I guess to the brothers, it is their way of helping me and making sure that I am happy and have a home. I do not have a home after losing my family and my husband.

I continue to look out over the land. I guess I do have a home, and here is my home. I see something moving in the distance; whatever it is, it is coming from the woods. I watch with great interest, and then it appears. The most beautiful wolf I have ever seen is in my eyesight. I know him. I remember this wolf. It is Alpha Maximus. He shifts back into a man and stands in the moonlight nude and beautiful. He looks up to the moon and arches his back. He lets out a beautiful howl. My wolf howls for him and wants him. MATE! My wolf is pacing and panting. Haven't we been through enough? The thought of a man or wolf or anyone touching my body makes me want to scream, but my wolf she longs for his touch. Go to him, and my wolf cries out, pushing me to go to him.

I cannot take it; I rush out of the bedroom and run through the house. I go out the front door and to the porch. I stand on the porch, and there he is, standing in front of me. He is beautiful as he looks at me in my long nightgown. He moves closer as both of us breathe hard and want one another.

"I ... I... I am afraid of being touched," I say. It is the only thing I can manage to get out as he moves so close to me. He stares into my eyes, and we are within an inch of each other. I cannot stop my breathing as it is heavy. I reach up and touch his face, but he respects my wishes and does not touch me. Tears begin to form and slide down my face. He reaches up to wipe away the tears but stops before he touches me.

"I will not hurt you," he whispers as he stands in front of me. He takes his thumb and wipes away the tears.

"I believe you," I say. He leans down, and his lips touch my lips. He kisses me and is so gentle. My wolf cries out for him.

"We should get you to bed. You need to rest and heal, little wolf," Alpha Maximus says.

"I agree," I say. I turn to walk away from him. My mate is right here in front of me. My wolf cries for him and wants him, but my body and my mind are not ready for that. I am screaming on the inside as I walk away from my mate. I make my way to the kitchen, and then I turn around to see him standing on the porch, looking out into the vastness of the woods. He is hurting too. This ordeal is not just my loss. It is his too. He lost his brother, and he brought his brother back here with my sister and his parents. He is in pain, and I need to recognize that he needs to heal too. I have to give him time to heal, and I need time to heal.

I start walking back to him. I want to tell him that I understand. As I make my way back to him, another wolf walks up to the porch. I stand in the door and listen to the wolves talking about perimeters and keeping watch. I have no idea about this type of thing. How will I take care of these wolves? There are only a few of us and all of this land.

"Alpha Maximus," I say as I walk back to him.

He turns around and looks at me. The moonlight hits his body just right, and my wolf is going insane for him, more than before; damn, he is unbelievably amazing.

"Yes, Luna Kayla," he says.

"Is everything okay?" I ask him.

He looks around at the woods. "Yes, other packs know that the numbers are down, and I am afraid someone will attack you. I do not have many wolves with me, but they are watching the perimeter. More of my wolves are on their way here to help," Alpha Maximus says.

"And when you leave me behind to go home, then what? Will this pack fall to an attack and another wolf, like Ranon, come in here and take me away or worse?" I ask him.

He looks down at the ground, and then it hits me. That is why he was running; he was thinking of how he would protect me and care for me as his mate. He is not sure how or what to do either. We are neither one ready for a mate, yet it has been thrown in our face. The decision is being made for us. Now he feels he should make sure I am taken care of not just because I lost my husband, his brother, but because I am his mate.

"Kayla," Alpha Maximus says, stopping to listen for something after he says my name. When he says my name, my entire body begins to shake and shiver, and I want to touch him. Why did this happen?

I move close to him and take his hand into mine for some reason. It feels incredible to hold his hand. "Kayla, I have several wolves that want to move south. It is cold during the winter, and they want to move to a southern pack. They are good wolves. They will be here tomorrow. They will help you and respect you. Most importantly, they will protect you," Alpha Maximus says.

"What will happen to you? Will you leave me? Are you rejecting me?" I ask him. Everything in his face seems to fade as I ask if he plans to reject me.

"I am not sure what we should do about this right now. You are my brother's wife, and," He says, but I stop him.

"I was your brother's wife. He was murdered," I say. I begin to cry and then lean into him. He puts his arm around me carefully as if he is unsure if he should touch me or allow me to just lay against him unbothered.

"I think we should see what happens, and I promise not to reject you unless you want me to reject you," Alpha Maximus says.

I look up into his eyes. "I am not sure what I want. My wolf is crying for you, and my body is destroyed. Why would any wolf want me? I am damaged, broken, and unloveable. I understand that you would not want a mate that has been with another wolf," I say.

He touches my face. "Do not ever say anything like that to me. Kayla, what happened to you was not your fault. Any wolf would be lucky to have you, even me. I am just not sure I want a mate. I have never thought about it or seriously thought it would not happen to me. I may be the Alpha of the pack, but I spend a lot of my time alone and away from everyone. I am not sure what I can offer you," Alpha Maximus says.

"Peace, you can offer me peace," I say to him.

"Why did you come back out here?" Alpha Maximus asks me.

"I was worried about you. I realized that you were in pain and that you had lost family. That maybe you needed someone to talk to, and I wanted to let you know that you can talk to me," I say.

"You are the first person to offer to listen to me. I guess everyone expects me to just be okay and move on after all of this. I am not sure how to move on, and I am hurting, Kayla, but I need to ... NO, I want to, not need to ... I want to make sure you are okay. It would mean everything to me if you were okay. I want something good to come from this, and I hope that is you. I am sorry, I am not making much sense," Alpha Maximus says.

"No, you are making perfect sense. I think I am going to bed now. Can we have breakfast together in the morning?" I ask him.

He smiles at me. "I would like that," Alpha Maximus says.

"Me too," I say.

Chapter 15 – A Million Reasons

Alpha Maximus POV

She is beautiful and perfect. I am a rugged Alpha. We do not live anywhere near one another. She has my brother's pack to run, and I will have to return home eventually. I do not deserve someone like her. She is too good for me. There are a million reasons why I cannot be with her and one why I should. She is my mate.

She told me I could give her peace, but can I? Can I offer her peace? Then what? Do I leave my pack and come here to be with her and help her rebuild everything here, or do I ask her to move and leave what little she has behind for me? Would I be that selfish of an asshole?

I have no idea how to handle this situation. No woman should get involved with me. I am poison. Kayla deserves so much more. She deserves a man like Soran was, and I am nothing like my brother. I have known all my life that I did not need a mate. It would be a disaster, just like it was with Nancy. I can still smell the fresh blood on her body. Her death was my fault. I have to tell Kayla the truth. The real reason I cannot be with her, but until then, I will show her the kindness she deserves, and maybe she will find a way to reject me and open the door for another mate.

"Alpha," Kayla calls to me. I turn to see her standing on the front porch. Her hair is washed and braided. She has taken the time to dress herself, and she even applied makeup.

"Wow, you look beautiful," I say as she walks toward me.

"I am sure my long nightgown and knotted hair were not very appealing," Kayla jokes.

I touch her face. Maybe, perhaps, we could be friends. She is so perfect. "Are you okay, Alpha Maximus?" Kayla asks me.

I shake off the feeling to pick her up and take her into my arms. My wolf begins crying for her. I take a deep breath and try to regroup, but it is becoming hard to think with her right here in front of me and looking so perfect.

"I am starting to think you are more afraid of me than I am of you," Kayla says.

"I do not want to hurt you, Kayla," I say a little more sternly than I meant to, but my words do not seem to faze her as she moves closer to me.

"I feel like we are in a game of cat and mouse. I have no idea what we should do, but we cannot avoid the fact we are mates forever. We are both suffering," Kayla says.

"How about that breakfast?" I ask her, changing the subject.

"I believe Char has breakfast ready for us. It will just be the two of us she has to go into town to do some shopping," Kayla says.

I will be alone with her. I hope I can control my wolf and my smart ass mouth. I do not want to hurt her feelings or make her feel uncomfortable in any way.

The two of us go into the house. Char leaves as we go into the kitchen. "Just leave everything. Jan should be here by the time you are finished, and she will do the cleaning, Miss Kayla. I mean Luna Kayla, forgive me. Do not try to clean or do any of our work, and we will handle it; you just focus on getting better," Char says as Luna Kayla and I take a seat at the table.

"Do not run away from me this time," I say as I sit across from her. She smiles at me, and her eyes seem to almost glow with her beautiful smile.

"I am afraid of being in love or having a mate," Luna Kayla says.

"We are going to focus on one thing at a time. First, your home, we have a lot of things to handle. You will be the Alpha of this pack, and it is important you understand your duties," I say.

She looks at me like an animal that has been cornered. "I did not realize I would have to be the Alpha of the pack," she says. She begins to breathe heavily and leans over.

I go to her and take her hand. "Everything will be fine. I have wonderful wolves coming to help you, and we will get you on track," I say.

She looks up at me with her beautiful eyes. "I am not an Alpha. I cannot lead the wolves. I only need a place to live and a pack to call home. Someone else can be the Alpha, not me," Kayla says.

"I had not thought this through. I am sorry. The land is yours, the pack is yours, but maybe someone else can be in charge. I will figure it out for you, okay. Just eat something for me," I say to her.

I am so close to her that the heat from her body and mine are melting together, and the scent is heavenly. I want to kiss her and hold her and so much more. My body and my wolf wants to take her to bed and make her ours, but I cannot touch her. I cannot be with her, and I cannot hurt her.

"Alpha," Kayla says so softly. I fight the urge, but I just cannot fight it anymore. I take her mouth, kissing her lips and pulling her to me with such force that our bodies collide, and I am on fire for her. I need to have her as mine. I need to be inside her and claim her. I want to mark her as my mate.

"Please stop," Kayla protests, but I do not let go; I push my tongue into her mouth and kiss her hard. I feel as if I need her; I want her. My wolf is going insane and needs her now. I touch her legs, and she screams. I let go of her, realizing I have royally fucked up as she runs away from me. I am poison. She deserves better than me.

She is screaming in the bedroom and crying. I sit at the breakfast table alone. I should not be here. I will leave when the wolves arrive. They can take over and help her get settled. I can take on this pack as mine and run it as Alpha from afar to protect her. It is the least I can do for her.

I could reject her, but she asked me not to reject her. Maybe when she is ready for someone else, then I can reject her, and she can move on with her. I am so sorry, Luna Kayla. I did not want to hurt you. The mate pull between us is stronger than anything I have ever felt in my life. I have to get away from her.

I go out the front door and run toward the woods. I will run and hide until dark. That way, I will not be drawn to her or hurt her in any way. I am sorry, Kayla. I am so very sorry.

I shift, running through the woods, taking my wolf form, and letting everything go. No worries, no troubles, and no mate to try to force into something she does not want. I get to a clearing, and I begin to hear Luna Kayla. I listen to her crying. "I fucked up. I should not have run from him," she is saying. Her thoughts are in my head. I wonder if she hears mine.

I am sorry, I whisper. Her thoughts go silent. "Alpha," I hear her say.

"Come to me, please," I say.

"I am coming to you. I am sorry," she says. I wait for her in the clearing.

I look up to see the most majestic wolf standing before me. I run to her, and we look at one another. We begin to nuzzle one another.

"Accept me as your mate, Alpha, please," she says.

I take a step back from her. Should I? "Why do you want me?" I ask her.

"I can see everything in your mind. I know what happened to your girlfriend and how she died. We are both broken, and maybe we can heal one another. Take me as your mate," Luna Kayla says.

"I thought you never wanted to be touched by a man again?" I asked her.

"I am not ready yet, but if you will wait on me, then I will be ready to be touched again someday, and when I am, I want it to be you," she says.

I nuzzle close to her and close my eyes. "Kayla, I accept you as my mate," I say to her.

I open my eyes and see tears coming down from her eyes and sliding down her beautiful fur.

"No more tears, only joy from now on, Kayla," I say to her.

"How about a run?" she says and takes off in front of me.

Chapter 16 - Secrets

There are decisions that need to be made about the pack and the pack land. I am the Alpha of the north pack lands, and I have responsibility. Do I let it go to one of my wolves and come here? Do I relinquish everything and be her mate and the Alpha of my father's pack? What is left of it? I must tell Marcus what is going on here. I cannot wait to hear what he will have to say.

I hear Char and Mallory talking with a few of the she-wolves that came down with my pack. She sounds happy, and she is laughing. Did I do that? Did I make her happy? I am not sure about that. Every time we sit down to try to eat a meal together, somehow I manage to upset her, but now maybe we can finally figure out this mate thing between us and move forward with rebuilding.

I pull my phone out of my pocket, and here goes nothing. I call Marcus. He picks up the phone and immediately begins screaming at me. "What the fuck are you doing?" he screams into the phone.

"I am not listening to this," I say. I hang up the phone. We can have that conversation later. My phone rings, and it is Marcus.

"Hello, brother," I say. He takes a deep breath.

"It is true that you are sleeping with your brother's wife?" he asks me.

"No, she can barely be in a room with someone, and she is still very fragile," I say. This is true, and I have not slept with her, only hold her hand and kissed her. My wolf begins thinking about her and growling. I cannot do this right now.

"Raymond told me that he saw you and Kayla hugged up together," Marcus says.

"I will be sending Raymond back to you today, number one. I do not need a spy. Got it? Number two, I did hold her when she was crying, not that I owe you an explanation about anything. Number three, I am thinking about moving back home and helping her run the pack because Marcus, Kayla is my mate!" I scream at him.

Marcus begins screaming and throwing a tantrum. "You do not deserve anyone after what you did to that poor girl, Nancy. That is why you were sent away permanently after your last visit home, was it not? You are poison Alpha Maximus, a murderer, and you do not deserve the pack land or Kayla. I doubt she is really your mate. Did you con her to get the pack land and use her?" Marcus screams.

Marcus will always hate me because he was friends with Nancy. He felt I killed her. I did not, but that is how he felt. If he only knew what really happened, he would know it was not my fault. And as far as never coming back, after that, I did not want to come back here. I had no reason to, but now I want to be here with her. I do not need to con anyone to get the pack land because I am the oldest, it is mine, but I am choosing to give it to Kayla as a gift.

I look behind me to see Luna Kayla standing behind me, crying. "She heard you. We are linked because we are mates," I say.

Marcus goes silent. "Goodbye, brother," he says.

Marcus hangs up the phone. Luna Kayla embraces me. "You are damaged more like me than I thought," she says.

She has no idea how badly I am damaged because of my parents and my brothers. I will never say anything bad about Soran to her. He was a good man, but there were dark things here and a dark moment when Soran could have turned down the wrong path, and I am sure I would have been blamed for it.

"I was thinking, if you are up for it, that maybe we could do something together, like a date. We should get to know one another if we are going to be mates, right?" I ask her. She smiles the biggest, most beautiful smile I have seen on her face since bringing her here with me. Her eyes are even smiling at me.

"A date? I do not think I have ever been on a date before. My parents were strict, and then I was promised to someone, so I did not date or ever really go anywhere," Luna Kayla says.

"Well, I can plan it. Is there anything that you would like to do that you have never done before?" I ask her. I can hear her thoughts, and her thoughts are running crazy.

"You know we have a lot of time to date and do things until you are ready to be my wife," I say. I stop. Did I just say that? Ready to be my wife? That is what will come next. I cannot just move in with her and expect her not to want to be married. I will have to marry her.

She touches my hand. "Do not be scared. We have a long time before we get to that point," she says.

Where did this amazing woman come from to be so loving and understanding after everything she experienced at the hands of that bastard Alpha? At that very second, I knew where I wanted to take her and what I wanted to do with her on our first date.

"I will take care of our first date, and you can handle our second date, deal?" I suggest. She smiles at me, leans into me, and kisses me on the lips. I look over as I take her into my arms and see Marcus's wolf, Raymond.

"I need to handle something," I say to Luna Kayla. I walk over to Raymond, who is standing at a distance. I extend my hand and shake it. He looks at me oddly. With my other hand, I ball up my fist and punch him in the face.

"Get the fuck back to Marcus and as far away from me as possible," I say. Raymond hits the ground, and I turn to walk away.

"I guess you forgot that Nancy was my sister, and you killed her," he says as I walk away. I turn back to him. I rush to him and pick him up by his collar.

"I did not kill your sister but believe what you want. Ask Marcus who her mate was and who killed her for rejecting him and choosing me. ASK MARCUS!" I scream at him. I drop Raymond on the ground.

"Why don't you tell me?" he asks me.

"Because I do not speak ill of the dead," I say. As I am walking away the second time, I remember that Luna Kayla can hear my thoughts. I hope she is not listening. I will tell her everything about Nancy someday, but it is not right for me to soil anyone's name right now. I will not do it.

Chapter 17 – I will do anything for your love

Luna Kayla POV

I walk away from Alpha Maximus to give him some space. One thing I know about pain is sometimes you just need everyone to leave you the hell alone. It is odd feelings someone else's pain. Alpha Maximus is broken and hiding behind his Alpha mentality, but I can see it, and I can feel it. From everything that I know about Soran and his parents; it seems so odd that they treated Alpha Maximus like he did not belong. I stop walking and turn back to see him. There is only one reason that I can think of that his father and brothers treated him differently. He is the oldest, yet he was sent away to be the Alpha of another pack and given to another man. He came back during the summer until the incident that he knew could harm one of his brothers. He is Soran's half-brother. It is the only thing I can think of that makes sense in this situation.

I will not ask him about it. I will not push him. He will tell me everything when the time is right. So why did he feel like he was the one obligated to care for me? He is an Alpha, yet he chooses to be my caretaker. He has a reason for choosing that. There is so much more to this amazing wolf than I know. I return to the house and watch out the window as he shifts and goes for a run. It seems to bring him peace when he runs. The other night when we ran together, we were both at peace. Maybe I should join him.

"Luna Kayla, Alpha Marucs is on the phone for you," Char tells me.

I walk toward the phone and then stop. "Tell him I have nothing to say to him," I say it loudly enough that I know he hears me. I start to walk away and Char reaches for me. She puts the phone to my ear.

"He is poison," Alpha Marcus says.

"FUCK OFF!" I say into the phone. I take the phone from Char and throw it onto the ground.

"DO not ever try to force me into a phone conversation or anything else again or I will have you taken to the edge of my property and dropped off. LET ME REPEAT THAT MY PROPERTY! I own this land!" I scream at her.

Char looks completely upset and distraught as I turn red in the face and growl. "I am sorry, he said it was important," Char says.

"My free will is more important than what Alpha Marcus wants, got it?" I ask her.

She shrinks beneath me. "I am sorry," Char says. For some reason I do not believe her apology. Maybe it would be better to leave her and go with Alpha Maximus let someone else have this place or let it rot. At this point I am not sure if being here is good for either of us.

I leave the cabin and start running toward the woods, shifting as I break the tree line. I growl into the woods, so Alpha Maximus knows that I am on my way to him. My wolf is happy and excited we are going to run with him again. She likes when we are with him. My wolf feels safe. Hell, I feel safe with him.

"Alpha Maximus," I howl out into the woods and then growl loudly. I hear him howling and start running toward him. The forest beneath my paws is wet and soggy but feels like heaven as I get closer to him. I finally reach him. I look up to see him waiting for me by a small pond. He looks majestic, maybe regal as I approach him. He is sexy in his wolf form. He turns to see me and his eyes meet mine.

"Luna Kayla," he says my name and it send chills down my spine. I take a deep breath as I shift back to my human form and stand in front of him nude and exposed. He looks me over, sniffs me and then returns to his human form in front of me. He takes me into his arms. Our skin touches one another and we are so close to one another.

"I cannot control myself around you if you are going to pop up nude, when my wolf is already going insane wanting to make you ours. I apologize now if I go further than you are ready, just give me a firm no when I go to far," Alpha Maximus says.

I touch his arm and then his bare chest. "I am not sure how far I can go. I am still healing," I say. I would give anything to be with you, but I am so afraid, but there is one thing I think we would be best for us. If you are willing to do it for me," I say.

Alpha Maximus looks at me strangely. "I am willing to do anything for your trust and love, Kayla. That is a lot for me. I did not want this, but you keep pulling me in and making me want to be a better wolf, a better person and be your mate. I know we have not known each other long and I am not even sure how this is possible but I know that I am in love with you. So Luna Kayla with that being said, I will do anything for your love," Alpha Maximus says.

"I think this land and your family are the poison and that we should go back to your pack," I say.

"You would do that for me," Alpha Maximus inquires. Like no one has ever done anything for him in his life.

"I would do anything for your love," I say, repeating back the words he said to me. Right now, all I can think about is being his in every way. I just need my body to heal so I can give him my body. I really want to give him my body. I never thought that would be possible. Every time I look into his eyes, I see something special. I see a future for us.

"I hate it here. This place haunts me, but I would give up everything to be with you. You will love the north pack territories. It is colder but the land is beautiful and the wolves are different than the wolves here. Things are less dramatic. We could build a life," Alpha Maximus says.

"Is there someone who can take this and be a good fit?" I ask. I am not sure I even care anymore, except for the fact that my sister is buried here. I do not want to be here either. I want to get as far away from the nightmare and the memories as possible.

"My Beta would be perfect and he would tell Marcus to fuck off," Alpha Maximus says.

I embrace him. Our bodies touch, skin to skin. My heart begins races and my breathing labored as he takes my chin lifts me to his lips and takes my mouth. "I want you," I whisper.

Chapter 18 – What is Marcus up to?

I look into his eyes. "I want you," I say as he holds me.

My want for him is unreal. I would love to be with him in every way, but I do not think I can right now. "I want you," I repeat as I bury my head into his chest.

"You have no idea how badly I want you, but not just sexually, Kayla. I want to be yours in every way. I want this to work," Alpha Maximus says.

He holds me in a way that makes me shiver. My body tingles and aches for him. "We will be together soon," I say.

"Do you really want to leave here?" Alpha Maximus asks me again.

I already answered his question once, but I think he is afraid I am leaving this pack because of fear. "Yes, I want to start a new life and forget every little bad thing that happened here," I say. His hand brushes through my hair. I am so close to him.

I look up into his eyes, my chin buried in his chest. "Kiss me," I whisper.

He leans down, takes my mouth, and kisses me. The sparks of our mate bond feel healing. Every touch from Maximus makes me want to be his in every way I can possibly be his. "I want to be as close to you as I can without judgment from everyone here. It feels like they all do not want us together. I feel ridiculed. Take me away from here today, please," I beg him.

"You can hand over the land to my Beta Al. He would honor the land and the legacy," Alpha Maximus says. He touches my chin. "You and I can leave immediately after Beta Al takes over."

I nod. "That is what I want. I want nothing more than to be your Luna. Are you sure you want someone broken?" I ask him.

Alpha Maximus looks upset. "You are not broken, and I never want to hear those words come out of your mouth. You are amazing, Kayla. You are my mate, my future wife, and Luna. You are not broken. You are perfect," Alpha Maximus says.

Snap. A twig snaps in the distance. "Someone is coming," I say.

"Go, I will catch up. I want to see who is listening to us and watching us," Alpha Maximus says.

I take my wolf form and begin running toward the house. My heart feels full and happy. I hear something or some wolf howling. That is not Alpha Maximus. I wonder who would be so interested in a conversation between me and Alpha Maximus. I also want to know why no one wants him to be happy.

I run toward the house, thinking. There are so many things I want to know about Alpha Maximus and his family. I did not know Soran as well as I thought I did after all. It seems there are a lot of secrets on this land, and to be perfectly honest, I do not

"

want to be a part of any of these secrets or lies. I had heard from a few people that Soran had a bit of a temper, but I had never seen anything but kindness from him and his family. Still, why did this family send one son away and treat him like garbage? Do I want to know the truth, or should I let it go and focus on building a life with Alpha Maximus?

I stop in front of the house. I can see two new she-wolves standing in the doorway of the house. I step up onto the porch. "Kayla?" one of the women asks me.

"Luna Kayla," I respond. I believe I earned the title.

"Sorry. I am June, and this is my sister Jana. We work for Alpha Marcus. He sent us to check on you and make sure Alpha Maximus is acting appropriately. I mean, you are aware he has a past and a dead girlfriend incident that haunts him. We do not want anything to happen to you, Luna," June says. She twists around in an odd fashion.

I smile at June and then turn to smile at Jane. "I appreciate you coming. Is Alpha Marcus with you?" I ask June.

"No, Luna Kayla. We are here in his place to check on you. I believe I already said that," June says sarcastically.

I lean into June. "Well, then you can get off my fucking porch and tell Alpha Marcus to go to hell," I say. I go into the house and slam the door, locking it behind me. June pulls at the door.

"He is crazy. He will hurt you just like he did Nancy. Be careful, Luna Kayla. Be very careful," June screams through the door.

I hear growling coming from outside and then screaming. Alpha Maximus! I rush to the door to see Alpha Maximus and a wolf I do not recognize fighting. The two women are trying to get into the house, but I will not let the two bitches inside. For all I know, they are working with the unknown wolf.

"Let us in!" June screams.

"NO!" I scream back at her.

Within a few minutes, Alpha Maximus manages to subdue the white wolf. He does not kill him, but the wolf is not moving. "Friend of yours?" he asks June and Jana as he walks past them.

The two rush over to the wolf to check on him. I open the door for Alpha Maximus. "We need to get the hell out of here, Kayla," Alpha Maximus says.

"I do not care what happens to this place. If your Beta wants it, then it is his. Otherwise, just get me out of here," I say. Alpha Maximus nods and pulls me to him. He kisses my forehead.

"I will gather my men and Beta Al. You pack anything you want to take, and we are out of here," Alpha Maximus says.

I rush up the stairs to grab a few things. Everything I am taking with me fits in a small bag. I do not want a lot to remind me of this horrible time in my life. I want to move on and be free from this place and this nightmare.

"Kayla," Alpha Maximus calls to me. I hear his heavy boots coming up the steps.

I step out of the bedroom with my bag. "I am ready," I say.

The two of us go down the stairs, waiting for me in the living room is Beta Al. "Do you want to be Alpha?" I ask him.

He looks puzzled. "Yes, Kayla," Beta Al answers.

"Then it is yours," I say. I grab Alpha Maximus and pull him out of the house. His wolves are following as I am dragging him away.

"Calm down. You are safe," Alpha Maximus says.

I hear wolves howling as Alpha Maximus, I, and three of his wolves get into one black SUV. I hope we are safe. I lean back on Alpha Maximus. I already feel relieved as we drive away.

Chapter 19 – What did Marcus do?

Alpha Maximus

Kayla lays on my shoulder and sleeps as Beta Dorian drives up north. She is snuggled into me and sleeping deeper than I have seen her sleep since rescuing her from Ranon. She is at peace. That is all I want for her, just peace. She may be right, and I can give her the peace she deserves. There is no one who deserves peace more than Kayla. She deserves the world. How will I ever give it to her?

Kayla opens her eyes for a moment and looks up at me. She smiles that beautiful smile of hers at me. "I can hear all of your thoughts, Alpha," Kayla says.

"Sorry," I say. Kayla closes her eyes and goes back to sleep. Maybe she was not as asleep as I thought she was.

I run my fingers through her hair and hold her close to me. How did I fall in love with her so quickly? Mate or not, she looks inside me and makes me feel whole and at peace. Kayla sees all the broken pieces inside me and wants to make me a better wolf.

I will sit Kayla down when we get home and tell her everything that happened. Kayla has to know the truth about what happened to Nancy. I do not want to stain Soran's name now that he is dead, but she has to know. Kayla opens her eyes and looks up at me again.

Kayla sits up and takes my hand. "I love you, Alpha Maximus, and that is all I need. I do not need to know anything except that we love one another and that we will always take care of one another," Kayla says.

"I do love you, Kayla, and I will care for you always," I say. I lean in and kiss her.

Beta Dorian hits the brakes hard, causing both of us to lean forward. Kayla hits her head on the seat in front of us. "Are you okay?" I ask her.

"Yes," Kayla says as she rubs her head.

I growl loudly. "What the hell is going on?" I ask Beta Dorian.

I look in front of us, and someone is blocking the road. It is three black SUVs. I get out of the truck to see my brother Alpha Marcus getting out of one of the SUVs. What the hell does he want? I know what he wants. He wants Kayla. I just don't understand why he is so worried about the land and Kayla.

"Hello, brother, what the fuck do you want?" I growl at him.

Beta Archie gets out of the SUV and joins me, leaving Dorian and Charlie in the SUV with Kayla to protect her. I do not trust Marcus. I know he is up to something.

"I want Kayla to give me the pack and the land. Then you can be on your way with her," Alpha Marcus says.

I narrow my eyes at him. I look back at Kayla. She is terrified. This confrontation is too much for her. "You are scaring her. Kayla has been through enough, and you are doing this to her? Why?" I ask him. I move closer to Marcus. I will kill him if he goes near Kayla.

Marcus moves closer to me. He is no match for me, and we both know it. I am bigger, stronger, and a lot angrier than he will ever be. I can snap Marcus like a twig, but I do not want to do that in front of Kayla.

Marcus stands before me, but he does not shrink before me. Instead, he looks at me, angry and arrogant. This display of arrogance is not my brother. What has happened to him? "I want that fucking land, Maximus!" Marcus demands.

I push Marcus back. He is too close and pissing me off. "It is not mine to give or Kayla's. There is a new Alpha. Go take it up with him," I growl at Marcus.

Marcus becomes furious. "What! You gave away my father's land! How could you?" Marcus is screaming at me. I am at a loss of why he suddenly gives a damn about the pack or the land.

"I am the oldest, not you! The land belongs to Kayla, and because you and your bullshit scared her, she wanted to leave. Why do you want it anyway?" I grab Marcus pulling him back to me. I want an answer, and he is going to give it to me.

The door opens on the SUV, and Kayla walks toward us. "Please stop," she is begging us both.

I let go of Marcus. "He will kill you, just like he killed Nancy. You are in danger with him. Mark my word Kayla, you will die if you stay with him," Marcus says as he backs away and gets into his truck.

Kayla rushes over to me. She stands close to me. Kayla trembles as fear runs through her body. "It is okay," I say to her. I notice her watching Marcus closely. Has she met Marcus? Does she know him? Our families were close, but how well did she know my brothers?

"I feel safer when I am close to you," Kayla says.

I lean down and kiss her forehead. "Let's go. We need to get home. We still have six more hours until we are home," I say to her.

Kayla stays close to me as we get back into the SUV. My mind races with thoughts of everything that has happened. The wedding, the kidnapping, how fast Marcus got to the pack lands, and how he knew where and when to find Ranon. Surely he was not involved in the murder of our brother, my parents, the entire pack, and what happened to Kayla.

I look down at Kayla, who is shaking now. I pull her into my arms and hold her. "I will not let Marcus hurt you," I whisper to her.

"Her already he has," Kayla says. She looks up at me, tears flowing from her eyes. What did he do?

Chapter 20 – Memories

Luna Kayla POV

Alpha Maximus is silent as we make our way home. Home seems like an odd thing to think about right now. I mean, where is my home? It is with Alpha Maximus, of course, but will Marcus try to destroy us? I think Marcus will do everything he can to hide his secret. I know a secret or two about Alpha Marcus. I have a secret about him, and I believe Alpha Maximus does too.

The SUV finally stops. I didn't think this trip would ever end. Alpha Maximus gets out of the SUV and is at my door quickly, and helps me out of the truck. He smiles at me and makes me feel like a princess. He is my knight in shining armor, after all. He saved me, not just from Alpha Ranon but from feeling broken.

"My lady," Alpha Maximus says. He reaches for my hand.

"Thank you, Alpha," I say. I take his hand.

The pack house is huge. I had heard that Alpha Maximus's north pack was huge, but judging by the size of this house, it is bigger than I imagined. "This is not our home," Alpha Maximus says.

He must have sensed my overwhelming feelings looking at the house. My mind is racing, thinking about how on earth I will be a Luna to such a huge pack. I hope they are all as kind as him.

"I bet your house is bigger," I tease him.

We step up onto a large porch. Alpha Maximus opens the door for me. "Actually, our house is smaller. So as you know, most of the wolves in this pack are kind and selfless. None of them are arrogant. We work together, and we play together. Well, except me. I stay to myself, but now that you are here, I guess I will need to be sociable," he says.

I don't get a chance to ask him about our home. She wolves surround us. "Oh my goodness, look at you. You are beautiful," one of them says. They are giggling and jumping over one another to get to me.

"I am Amy, this is JayJay, Georgia, and PJ," Amy says. They are all so excited to meet me, and it is a bit overwhelming.

One of the Beta wolves calls Alpha Maximus, and he leaves me for a moment. "I will be right back," Alpha Maximus says, kissing me on the cheek and going into an office with two beta wolves. Something is up. I can feel it.

The She wolves are all over me. "We are so happy you are here with us. Alpha Maximus needs someone, and you are so perfect," Jay Jay says.

"Thank you. He is very kind," I say. I am not sure what to say or how much they know about what happened to me. Honestly, I do not want to ever talk about the past again. I know I will have to talk about it eventually to Alpha Maximus but not today and not with the she wolves.

Amy pulls me toward the kitchen. "Come with us. I know you are hungry," she says. The she wolves take me into the kitchen to feed me and talk. I sit down at a large table.

"This is where we eat after we cook. Jay Jay and I cook for the pack every night. Well, not all of the pack, just Alpha Maximus, the betas, and a few single wolves. Most of the men are married, but there are a few that come here to eat," Amy says.

Georgia hands me a cup of hot tea. I hear a loud growl from the front office. "OH SHIT!" Amy says. She looks over at me. "Alpha Maximus is pissed off," she says.

"We saw Marcus on the way here," I say. Maybe I should not have said anything, but I did.

Amy sits down beside me. "Do you know Marcus?" she asks me.

I nod. "I do," I answer.

Amy shakes her head. "Alpha Marcus is a bad man, and so is the other one, Alpha..." Amy stops. Jay Jay punches her lightly.

"Sorry I was out of line," Amy says.

"It is fine. I prefer people to speak their minds — no need to sugarcoat anything around me. I have heard it, seen and been through it," I say with a smile. I sip my tea.

"We are sorry," Georgia says. I can see the pain in her eyes. She is sorry for me, but there is no need to be. I am fine.

The she wolves sit down with me quietly. We all sip our tea. PJ sets some cookies on the table for us and joins us. The quiet becomes too much for me. "Tell me, Georgia, are you married?" I ask her because she is the closest one to me at the moment.

"No, I was. My husband passed away, and Alpha Maximus gave me a place to stay. My pack was slaughtered. I was one of the few survivors," Georgia says. I am sorry I asked, but I know how she feels. I reach for her hand and hold it in mine.

"I am sorry," I say.

Amy leans over the table to get a little closer to me. "This pack is built on misfits. We all either did not fit in with our pack, or our packs were murdered. Alpha Maximus gives us hope. That is why we are all so excited he found his mate. No one is more deserving than Alpha," Amy says.

His pack loves him. They trust him. I watch wolves coming in and out of the pack house; each of them is so kind to me. They speak to me, welcome me to the pack, and talk kindly of Alpha Maximus. Alpha Ranon was wrong about no one ever wanting me. I am accepted here. This is my home.

"You are smiling," Alpha Maximus says. I look up to see him standing beside me. I was so deep in thought that I had not noticed him walking into the dining room.

I quickly stand up and kiss him. "I was thinking about how I belong here. Your pack is wonderful. Thank you for bringing me here," I say excitedly.

There is something wrong I can tell he is trying to hide it. "We need to talk," Alpha Maximus says. His arm is firmly on my waist. I begin to shake.

"What is wrong?" I ask him.

"Marcus attacked the pack lands and killed Alpha Al. The few wolves that were there are all dead," Alpha Maximus tells me.

He was planning to kill me, but I already knew that. I knew he wanted me to die at the hands of Alpha Ranon. It was Alpha Marcus that helped Alpha Ranon.

"I can hear your thoughts, Kayla. How did you know Alpha Marcus was helping Alpha Ranon?" he asks me.

Alpha Maximus is still holding me tightly. His betas are coming in closer to hear what I have to say. "Because I saw him the night of my wedding and again at the pack house when I was in the dog cage," I say. I begin to tremble.

Alpha Maximus pulls me close to him. My thoughts are racing with the pack house of painful memories. "Stop," he says. He sees my memories, and then I focus on Marcus standing there, watching them hit me and beat me. "Stop," Alpha Maximus says again. I try to stop the thoughts, but they are coming so fast.

"That is how he got here so quickly and why he did not need me to pick him up at the airport. I will kill him for all of this," Alpha Maximus growls.

Chapter 21 – Little Cabin

Luna Kayla POV

I can see pain and anger rising inside Alpha Maximus. He is furious with Alpha Marcus as he scans my memories. I try to stop all the memories as they flood my mind, but I cannot stop them.

"Show Kayla her new home. I will be there soon," Alpha Maximus says to Amy. He is still holding my waist tightly. I kiss his lips and lay my head on his chest just for a moment to offer him comfort. He is in a lot of pain.

"Is it alright if Georgia comes with me too?" I ask as Alpha Maximus lets go of me.

"Yes, take the three she wolves. They can show you around. I have some things to take care of, but I promise to be home soon," Alpha Maximus says.

"Okay, but do not leave me alone my first night here. We need to talk before you take off after your brother, please, Alpha," I say. Alpha Maximus nods and turns away from me.

The three she wolves gather around me as we leave the pack house. "We can walk. It is a nice walk to the Alpha's house," Jay Jay says.

The door opens behind us, and a male wolf comes up to Amy. "The Alpha wants me to keep an eye on the four of you," he says. He looks happy to go with Amy.

"This is Beta Rocky," Amy says to me. I look at his hand, and there is no wedding ring. I notice he is really close to Amy. They are both smiling and acting in a way that lets me know they are more than friends. Hmmm, something is going on there. Good for Amy.

"Sure, I promise not to be any trouble," I say.

Jay Jay, PJ, Georgia, and I walk in front of Amy and Rocky. I do not look back, but PJ does occasionally. "There are such a cute couple," PJ says.

I look back to see them closer than before, and when Amy sees me watching her, she moves away from Beta Rocky. "Is there some reason the two of them cannot be together? Am I missing something?" I ask.

It gets quiet between the three of us for a moment. "Beta Rocky needs Alpha Maximus's permission to see Amy because she was the former Alpha's niece," Georgia says.

"Okay then, why doesn't he just ask him?" I ask.

"Because Alpha Maximus is very protective of Amy. Her parents were killed. He has kept an eye on her most of her life," Georgia says.

We continue our walk to my new home. We finally make it to the small cabin. "I love it," I say.

"Wait until you see the inside. Amy keeps it clean and well-stocked, but you can do that or let her continue. That is up to you," PJ says.

I step onto the porch and open the door to my new home. I am excited and nervous. The she wolves follow me into the small cabin. The house is cute, well-decorated, and immaculate. Not the norm for a bachelor wolf, especially not a bachelor Alpha, but there is nothing ordinary about Alpha Maximus and his kindness.

Beta Rocky stays on the porch to keep watch. Amy comes into the house to show me around. "I changed the sheets on the bed and did all the laundry while Alpha Maximus was south helping you. By the way, where are your things?" Amy asks me.

"I don't have anything. I will need clothes and everything," I say, taking a deep breath. Everything I had is gone except the few things that Char made me.

"I have some clothes your size. We can chip in together and give you some of our things for now," PJ says.

I hug PJ. The other she wolves join us in a group hug. "Thank you so much for helping me," I say. I begin to cry, happy tears.

"We are just happy you are here with us," Amy says.

I will help Amy and Beta Rocky by speaking with Alpha Maximus. Not today, but soon, when things die down a little bit. "I am happy to be here with you all. I hope you will help me plan my wedding," I say.

"Oh my gosh, when? How soon?" Georgia is going crazy, jumping up and down.

"Soon, we want to be married as soon as possible," I say. This time I will marry forever to my mate, not someone I am forced to marry or someone to protect my pack, but a man who loves me and wants to be with me and only me.

There is a loud noise on the front porch. "Beta Rocky!" Amy calls out to him. She runs to the front door and opens it. Beta Rocky is lying on the porch, not moving. Amy rushes out the door to pull him into the house.

I look across the path and see Alpha Marcus. What the hell does he want? He took the pack land, and he killed the wolves. What else could he want?

SHIFT AND RUN! I hear Alpha Maximus in my mind link. "We have to shift and run!" I tell them.

Amy is pulling Beta Rocky into the house. "Go, Luna Kayla. I will not leave Rocky. I love him," she cries.

"I am not leaving you or him," I say. The four of us pick up Beta Rocky and carry him to the back of the house. Amy stays with him in the spare bedroom.

"We have to fight," I say.

"I am ready," Georgia says.

"Me too," PJ says.

"And Me," Jay Jay says.

I am coming, Kayla. Don't do anything to get yourself killed! I hear Alpha Maximus in my mind link.

"Alpha Maximus is almost here," I say.

The door opens, and it is Alpha Marcus. "I tried to warn you Luna Kayla. Getting involved with my brother would get you killed, but you are a dumb bitch just like that little whore Nancy," Alpha Marcus says.

"You killed here, didn't you, not Alpha Maximus?" I ask him.

Alpha Marcus moves closer to me. He is here to kill me. "No, sweetie. It was Soran, but I did push him to it. I guess it was my fault," Alpha Marcus says.

Alpha Marcus keeps moving closer until he is at the kitchen entrance. There is nowhere really for us to go, except the back bedroom and then what.

"Why do you want to kill me? Why did you kill your family, my family, the pack?" I ask him. At this point, no matter what he says, I do not want to hear, but I am stalling to give Alpha Maximus time to get to me.

"Because Kayla, you were supposed to be mine first, but your father said no, that you were too young, but then promised you to my brother. I decided the best way to make you pay was to give you to Alpha Ranon and take the pack land, but then here comes my brother, the murderer, to save the day, and you just had to be his damn mate! You little bitch!"

Alpha Marcus is furious. He comes running toward me and shifts into his wolf. "How did it feel when Alpha Ranon raped you? I heard you scream for Soran," Alpha Marcus taunts me.

I grab a kitchen knife and stab him as hard as I can in his face. Alpha Marcus growls and bites me. "SHIFT, KAYLA!" Alpha Maximus growls.

The bite is painful. I try to shift, but Alpha Marcus bites me again. Alpha Maximus bites Alpha Marcus and pulls him off me. Alpha Maximus is shaking Marcus. I am screaming from the pain in my arm. Georgia helps me to the back of the house.

PJ, Georgia, Jay Jay, and I hide in the spare room across from Amy and Beta Rocky. We can hear the fighting, growling, and yelping. Please let my Alpha come out alive. I am hurt, and I cannot help him.

I hear more wolves howling and coming into the cabin. "I am scared," I say.

"Us too," PJ says. We are huddled together when the house goes silent. We are breathing heavily and terrified when the door creaks and opens to the bedroom door.

"Kayla," Alpha Maximus says.

I get up and rush to him. He is in his human form and hurt. He falls onto a bed in the room. "Marcus is dead," He says softly.

"Rest and heal, my love," I say. I lay beside him.

"I will get the pack doctor for him and Beta Rocky," Georgia says and rushes out the door for help.

One of the Beta wolves comes to the door. "Stay in here until we clear out the bodies," he says.

"Okay," I say. I lay my head on Maximus and hold him. I will not leave him or let go. I kiss him as I begin to cry. I do not want to lose you, Max. Please be okay.

Chapter 22 – Love heals the deepest wounds

Luna Kayla POV

I stayed with my Alpha, not leaving his side. I want to be here every moment until he is fully healed. Amy stayed with Beta Rocky across the hall from me. PJ and Jay Jay stayed with us, helping us feed and care for Beta Rocky and my Alpha day and night. It was a slow healing process for Beta Rocky and Alpha Maximus.

Alpha Maximus took on several larger wolves in the fight to save me. Even with his mighty pack, he was hurt badly. I have seen fighting before, and I have seen wolves hurt but seeing my sweet Alpha hurt was too much for my heart. I think I cried every tear in my body out as I lay beside him.

"Kayla," Alpha Maximus whispers.

I raise my head and look at him. My mind had fallen into a semi-deep sleep waiting for the moment he opened his eyes and fussed at me for doting on him.

"I am here, Alpha Maximus. I am here with you," I say. I take his hand and hold it tightly, then lean up and kiss his sweet lips.

"How long have I been out?" Alpha Maximus asks.

"Three days, but you are healing and should be on your feet soon," I say.

Alpha Maximus begins to move around. He groans as he moves to the side of the bed. "I need to let the pack know that I am okay. Is Beta Rocky overseeing the pack?" Alpha Maximus asks.

I shake my head. "No, he is hurt badly. Amy is with him. She is caring for him," I say. I am not sure if that is something I should tell him right now. My mind flashes to the two of them laughing and holding hands. I smile.

Alpha Maximus laughs. "I know more going on in my pack than they think I know, Kayla. I know all about Amy and Beta Rocky. There is nothing to hide, but if he wants to go any further, he needs my permission," Alpha Maximus says.

I huff at Alpha Maximus. "You know something? I understand pack etiquette, but you should just give him permission to be with her. He loves her. I can see it," I say.

Alpha Maximus puts his arm around. "Maybe I will, but first, I have something else on my mind," Alpha Maximus says.

Alpha Maximus looks a little nervous and maybe shy. He almost looks like a boy about to kiss a girl for the first time. "What is it?" I ask him, grinning from ear to ear, waiting for what is on his mind.

The only thing that should be on his mind is healing and getting back to his pack. I should not even be in the equation, but I have a feeling that whatever is on his mind has to do with me.

"I love you, Kayla. I want you to tell me everything, and then I want us to start over. Marcus is gone. He cannot hurt you. Ranon is gone. He cannot hurt you, either. I have made sure that you are protected. Now I need you to trust me with what happened to you, so we can both heal," Alpha Maximus says.

I sit on the side of the bed for a moment. "Okay, but you must tell me the truth about Soran and Nancy. I need to know everything, and then we can both move on and put all of it behind us. I do not want any secrets in our marriage, only love and respect for one another," I say.

Alpha Maximus sits silently for a moment. "I know I am asking you for a lot. You do not have to relive every detail. Just let me help you heal, and you can help me, too," Alpha Maximus says.

"Okay, but I want to tell you everything. I do not want to skip any part because you will not understand if I am not honest. The same goes for you. I have to know everything no matter how hard it is," I say.

I fall into his arms. I lay my head on his healing chest and listen to him breathe. I listen to his heart beating, and I feel nothing but love for him. Peace, this is so peaceful. I have a feeling there is so much more peace to come for us.

The door opens, and someone knocks softly. I look up to see Amy. "I am sorry to bother you. I thought I heard Alpha Maximus talking. I only wanted to see how he is feeling," Amy says.

"Come in and sit with me," Alpha Maximus says.

I stand up. My plan is to leave Alpha Maximus and Amy to talk. "Do not leave. This involves you, my future Luna," Alpha Maximus says. I quickly sit back down and wait for Amy to take a seat on the chair next to the bed.

"Have I done something wrong, Alpha?" Amy asks. I can see her mind racing. She is worried about her relationship with Beta Rocky.

"No, Amy. You have done nothing wrong, but we need to discuss your relationship with Beta Rocky and the next steps," Alpha Maximus says. He moves to stand. I can see that he is still in pain from the multiple wolf bites from Marcus and his men.

If Alpha Maximus was hurt this bad, I have to wonder what Marcus and his wolves looked like when the fight was over. I was not allowed out of the bedroom while they cleaned up the carnage, but I am guessing it was terrible.

"I am sorry, Alpha. If you want me to leave the pack, I will, but I love him. Please do not punish Beta Rocky. I made the advance on him," Amy begins to cry.

Alpha Maximus moves closer to her. "Have I ever punished anyone for being in love? Have I ever denied you the right to date? I am charged and blessed with looking out for you. You are not my prisoner. Have I ever mistreated anyone in this pack?" Alpha Maximus questions her.

Amy is still shaking. "No, but I was the niece of the Alpha, and I know it is a serious offensive to be involved with me without permission from the Alpha. I am sorry, please," Amy continues to cry.

"You do not need my permission to be in love. If you love him and it is serious, then you have my blessing to be with him. Is it serious? Does he love you?" Alpha Maximus asks Amy.

She wipes the tears away from her face. "We want to get married, but we are both afraid that you would say no or banish us from the pack," Amy says.

Alpha Maximus becomes upset. He moves back over to the bed and sits down. He is looking at Amy, and he is angry with her. "When have I ever banished anyone from this pack or done anything like that? Have I not always been an open and honest Alpha?" Alpha Maximus questions her.

Amy sits quietly for a moment. She thinks about what Alpha Maximus is saying. "I know, but we were worried. I guess we should've just come to you instead of sneaking around," Amy says. She looks at me strangely. She thinks I told him.

"She did not tell me. I have known for a few months now. I knew the weekend of the pack's summer celebration. I saw the two of you by the river, and I knew then. I waited for you to ask me, but it never happened. So do not blame Kayla," Alpha Maximus quickly defends me.

Amy stands up and moves close to Alpha Maximus. She puts her arms around him to hug him. "Thank you, Alpha. I cannot wait to plan my wedding," Amy says.

She stops at the bedroom door and looks back. "Beta Rocky still has to ask for your permission, doesn't he?" Amy asks.

Alpha Maximus looks at me and then back to Amy. "You know, since I am not feeling well, he can ask Kayla for permission. I give her the right to make decisions until I feel better, but Amy, Beta Rocky will be a part of our family, and he needs to overcome his fear of me. I would appreciate it if he respected you enough to ask me," Alpha Maximus says.

Amy stands at the bedroom door for a moment. "You are right. We should respect you and value our relationship enough to ask," Amy says. She leaves the bedroom and goes across the hall.

"How is he?" Alpha Maximus asks.

"He is hurt badly. I hope he makes it. The pack doctor said there was a lot of damage, and his wolf is healing very slowly. I can relate to that," I say.

Alpha Maximus pulls me close to him. "How did you heal after everything that happened to you?" he asks.

"You helped me heal, and Amy will do the same for Beta Rocky," I say.

"Love always heals, even the deepest wounds," Alpha Maximus says.

Chapter 23 – 3 weeks later

Luna Kayla POV

Three weeks after the attack by Alpha Marcus, everyone seems to be back to normal. Alpha Maximus continues to dote on me and make me sweet promises. I think it is time for me to fulfill my promise. I have to tell him everything starting with what happened at the pack house of pain.

Amy helps me prepare dinner for Alpha Maximus and myself for the night. She knows all his favorite things and is happy to help me make this night special. I am not that great of a cook, and I want tonight to be perfect. I have a lot to do before tonight.

"Where is Beta Rocky while you are helping me?" I ask Amy.

Amy looks really nervous. "Well, he is asking Alpha Maximus if he can marry me. I am so nervous I cannot think," Amy says. She drops the lid to the pan on the floor and starts crying.

I rush over to help. "It is fine. Alpha Maximus already said you could get married. Alpha Maximus wants you to be happy," I reassure her.

Amy is distraught. "I know, but things are a little more complicated now, and if he says no, I will be a single mother," Amy cries.

Amy sits down on the floor, crying and holding the lid to the pan. I sit down beside her and take the pan. I toss it into the sink to wash. "You're pregnant. That is great," I say, smiling and hugging her.

Amy shakes her head. "What if Alpha Maximus has changed his mind? I mean, it's been three weeks since he told me okay. Beta Rocky wants to do things right. He loves this pack and me. He does not want to disappoint anyone, especially not Alpha Maximus, not after everything Alpha did for Rocky," Amy says.

I lean back against the kitchen cabinet. "Alpha Maximus helped Beta Rocky, too, didn't he?" I ask. I already know the answer.

"Yes, his family was murdered. I told you we are all the unwanted here, just like Alpha. His family never wanted him, but that is for him to tell you. He gave us all hope. We all want to please him. I hope my getting pregnant doesn't upset him," Amy says.

I take Amy's hand and hold it for a moment. "You know this is wonderful news. I think he will be very happy for both of you. I can help plan your wedding and baby shower," I say, trying to change the conversation to joy instead of sadness.

Amy and I begin to laugh and talk about a wedding. "What about your wedding? Any idea when?" Amy asks me.

"Soon," I answer. The same thing I keep telling Alpha Maximus. We sleep in separate beds, and I change the subject of marriage when he brings it up, but it is time

I say yes and set a date. I plan to do that tonight. I plan to make everything right tonight.

"How soon?" I look to see Alpha Maximus with Beta Rocky standing at the kitchen door.

"Soon," I repeat. Alpha Maximus lets out a low growl. I am sure I frustrate this man, but he follows the growl with a sweet smile. So I know he is not angry with me.

"Alpha Maximus," Amy quickly stands. She looks at the stove boiling over and starts trying to clean up.

"Leave it. I got this," I say.

"Come with me," Alpha Maximus says to her. I clean the mess up in the kitchen and turn everything down on low so that I can join the conversation.

I walk into the living room, and everyone looks so serious. "We were waiting for you," Alpha Maximus says.

I sit down next to Alpha Maximus. Beta Rocky and Amy look terrified. It is not terror, and it is more the want to please and respect their Alpha. The two of them are so afraid of Alpha Maximus being disappointed.

"Beta Rocky tells me that the two of you want to get married soon because you are expecting. I cannot allow that. If you want to marry because you love one another, that is fine. Please be happy, but if you are only getting married because you are pregnant, then the answer is no," Alpha Maximus says.

His face is dead serious. I see it. I see his mother. His thoughts are on her. She married because she was pregnant, and that is why she hated him. Alpha Maximus does not want the same for Amy.

Amy and Beta Rocky look at one another. She smiles at him with the sweetest smile. "I love him more than I love myself, and I hope he feels the same," Amy says.

Beta Rocky takes Amy's hand. "I do. I wanted to marry you before we found out you were pregnant. This is just a bonus," Beta Rocky says.

The two of them look so happy and in love. I wonder what it will feel like to become pregnant by the man I love. First, I have to have sex with him. My thoughts run crazy with Alpha Maximus touching me and kissing me.

Alpha Maximus leans over and kisses my cheek. "Soon," he says. He gives me my answer for everything.

"Then it is decided. Welcome to the family, Beta Rocky," Alpha Maximus says.

"There is one more thing," I say.

"What is that?" Amy asks.

"I think I burned the food," I say, looking at the smoke coming from the kitchen.

"I got it," Amy says. Amy and Beta Rocky rush into the kitchen to clean up the mess.

"I am not a good cook or housekeeper," I say. I lean my head over on Alpha Maximus.

Alpha Maximus laughs. "Neither am I. Maybe we could all go out to dinner. You have not been into town. There is a great place I can take you. We can celebrate Amy and Beta Rocky getting engaged," Alpha Maximus says.

"That would be nice," I say.

I go into the kitchen and help Amy and Beta Rocky. I watch Alpha Maximus enter the front bedroom while the three of us clean up the mess. "I am sorry. I should've been watching the food," I say.

"It is fine," Amy says.

Amy and Beta Rocky are both looking behind me. I turn to see Alpha Maximus. "You were right. There is one more thing, Kayla. Will you be my wife?" he asks me as he goes to one knee and opens a small ring box.

My heart is racing as I drop the dish towel I am holding and walk over to Alpha Maximus. All of his kindness flashes through my mind: every kind word and gesture dances around in my heart.

"Yes," I answer him.

Alpha Maximus slides the small heart-shaped diamond onto my finger. My heart is so full. He stands and takes me into his arms. His embrace heals every broken piece inside me. I love this wolf.

Chapter 24 – I am ready

Alpha Maximus POV

"Come with me," Kayla says.

She is looking at her ring finger and smiling. I wonder what she needs to say that she wants to be alone. She steps out onto the front porch and continues holding my hand.

"I want to go for a run," Kayla says.

"What about our double date with Beta Rocky and Amy?" I ask her. Not that I am complaining. I would much rather be alone with her than go on a double date with Beta Rocky and Amy.

"If it is okay with you, I really want to celebrate just the two of us tonight," Kayla says.

"I will tell them," I say. I do not get the chance. Beta Rocky and Amy come outside and see us talking. Maybe they took the hint, or maybe they wanted to be alone too.

"We were thinking this has been an exciting night, and we can go out another night to celebrate," Amy says. She looks at Kayla and gives her this look of understanding. One thing about Amy and Kayla is that they seem to click and know each other well.

"Maybe another night. We can get together tomorrow to discuss our wedding plans. We have a lot to do," Kayla says, smiling and glowing. She is excited to be my wife. Seeing her this happy puts me over the moon.

Amy rushes over to Kayla, and the two embrace, giggling and talking about the things they want for their wedding. Beta Rocky and I give the two brides-to-be a moment to gush over their soon-to-be nuptials.

"We should go," Amy calls out to Beta Rocky, and he follows her.

"Good Night, Alpha Maximus. Good Night, Luna Kayla," Amy and Beta Rocky say.

We watch them leave and hold hands as the sun goes down over the trees. "Do you still want to go for a run with me?" I ask Kayla.

"There is something else I want from you, Alpha Maximus," Kayla trembles as she speaks. She wants us to be together. I do not want to push her. We have our entire lives ahead of us, but I will not deny her either. I cannot lie. I want to touch the woman I love. I have been waiting for the moment she allows me to make love to her.

I pull her closer to me and take her mouth. I kiss her deeply. Her breathing is labored as I hold her waist. "We can wait," I say. I want her to have the option to wait. I understand everything she has been through and will wait as long as she needs me to.

"No, I want to be with you. I want it to happen tonight. I want to feel you close to me. I want to feel love from you in every way. I want you inside me," Kayla says.

My mind is spinning in a million places. I want this to be beautiful and something she enjoys, not something that makes her relive a horror from the days she was with that bastard. Instead, I want this to be perfect. I want her to feel loved.

"You are overthinking," Kayla says.

"I know, but the thought of hurting you in any way is not what I want," I say.

"Are you planning to hit me or force yourself on me? Of course, you are not. So let's just spend the night together and see what happens," Kayla says. She smiles that beautiful smile of hers at me. I want her now.

My wolf is going insane. My wolf is ready to mate with her and take her to bed. If I said I do not want to touch every part of her body, I would be a liar.

I pull her close to me. "You are everything to me," I say to her. I swoop her into my arms and carry her back into the house. I will make love to her. I will be gentle, and I will take my time with her. She will love every minute of everything that happens between us.

I take her into my bedroom. She has not shared a bed with me since she has been here. I have not bothered her or made a fuss. I have given her all the space she needs, but she will sleep with me in my bed tonight. Tonight I will claim her as mine. Every night after tonight we will share a bed together and be lovers.

I lay her in the bed and climb in the bed beside her. I lay with her, taking her mouth and kissing her. I let my hand wander her body as she breathes hard and moans.

I unbutton her top and release her breast from her bra. Her breasts are beautiful. I kiss down her chin to her breast. I take one of her nipples into my mouth and begin to suck. Kayla arches her back as I suck one nipple and play with the other. She is enjoying herself, and that is what I want.

I move down her body and remove her pants and panties. I remove my shirt but not my pants yet. I push her long sexy legs apart as I kiss down to her pussy. I kiss her mound and move to her wet sweet spot. Kayla moans as I let my tongue work to make her feel good.

Kayla moans and squirms from my tongue. She gathers the sheets in her hands, and her body begins to shake. She is cumming for me. "Oh, Maximus!" Kayla moans. This is what I want. I want her to enjoy everything that happens tonight.

I taste her sweet juices as she drips from her massive orgasm. I lick her up to her clit and begin sucking her clit, not too hard but hard enough to send her into overdrive. "Again," she moans.

I kiss up her stomach, teasing her as my tongue licks her nipples and then her neck. I take her mouth with her sweet taste still on my tongue. She moans and wraps her legs around me. I push my hard cock still inside my pants against her.

"I want you, please, Maximus. I am ready," Kayla moans.

I kiss her sweet lips. "I am ready, too," I say. I am ready. I am ready to take her now.

Chapter 25 – Peace

Kayla POV

Alpha Maximus has brought me to ecstasy multiple times, orgasm after orgasm. I want him to fuck me now. His tongue is heaven, and I bet his cock will be too. "I am ready," I moan.

Alpha Maximus gets out of the bed. I watch him as he removes his pants. His cock is at attention and ready for me. I lick my lips and move to the side of the bed. I touch his hip and pull him to me. I want his cock in my mouth.

"YES," he moans as I take him into my mouth. He touches the back of my head but doesn't try to force anything. Alpha Maximus is enjoying himself as I please him. I want nothing more than to please him in every way possible.

Alpha Maximus pulls back from me, and I kiss the tip of his cock. I don't know why, but it felt like the thing to do in the heat of the moment. Alpha Maximus moves toward me, easing me back onto my back. He is on top of me, and our lips touch. His kiss is so gentle.

Both of us are breathing heavily as he kisses me. I moan when I feel the tip of his cock at my entrance. Alpha slides into me slowly. My body tingles and wants him. Damn, I want him! No matter what happened before, the here and now are important. I want to be his wife, his luna, and his lover. To be his lover, I have to let my guard down and surrender myself to him.

Alpha Maximus enters me. My body begins to quiver. "Mark me as your mate," I moan.

Alpha Maximus pushes deep inside me. He kisses my neck. I think about how painful the last mark was, but this mark will be a joyous mark. I want to be his mate. "Mark me, please," I beg him, moaning as his hard cock slides in and out of me.

Alpha Maximus releases his wolf fangs and bites into my chest. I scream. "ARRGGG!" Tears begin to slide down my face as his sharp teeth penetrate my skin. I close my eyes and focus on the pleasure of his cock sliding in and out of me. I moan as he completes his mark.

"You are mine now," Alpha Maximus says.

"I always will be yours," I say. Alpha Maximus takes my mouth. Our tongues dance as our bodies bring pleasure to one another. Alpha Maximus slides in and out of me. His rhythm is perfect. My walls tighten, and my body shivers with delight.

"Cum for me," Alpha Maximus says.

Alpha Maximus kisses down to my nipple. He takes my nipple into his mouth and gently bites me as he thrusts harder inside me. "Harder," I moan.

Alpha Maximus increases his rhythm, pushing me to my limits as he takes me. "I am cumming for you," I moan. My body tingles as he fucks me harder.

"I want to fuck you," I say. Alpha Maximus kisses me, pulls out of me, and rolls onto his back.

I mount my Alpha, sliding his cock inside my wet, slick pussy. I begin to move back and forth, taking him deep inside me. His hands are on my hips, guiding me as I fuck him. I feel as if I am going to explode again.

I increase my speed, fucking him faster and faster, wanting him to fill my pussy with his cock juice. Alpha Maximus pushes up, groaning as his cock rams deeper inside me. "Make me cum," I moan.

He pulls me close to him, taking my nipple into his mouth. I bounce faster, wanting him harder. I begin to cum. I moan and scream out his name. "MAXIMUS cum with me," I plead with him.

Alpha Maximus explodes inside me. I continue sliding on his cock until I feel him go limp. I lay my head on his chest. "That was perfect," I whisper. I kiss his chest.

His hand is on my back, rubbing me, and then he kisses my forehead. I love his forehead kisses. "I love you," Alpha Maximus says.

"I love you too," I say.

We lay like this for a while, naked and holding one another. I feel like I am going to fall asleep when my sweet Alpha begins moving beneath me. "I want to hold you and check your mark," Alpha Maximus says.

I move to lie beside him. Alpha Maximus carefully checks my mark. "Does it hurt?" Alpha Maximus asks.

I nod. "Yes. It hurts bad. Let me bite you," I say.

"Bite me if that will make us even," Alpha Maximus says, smiling. He continues to examine the mark.

"I don't want to bite you. You can make it up to me in other ways," I say, pulling him close to me. I want him again and again. My wolf is going crazy for him.

Alpha Maximus leans forward and kisses me. "I can handle that," Alpha Maximus says.

"Do we have to have a big wedding?" I ask him as he kisses my neck.

Alpha Maximus stops and looks me in the eye. "We will have whatever you want. Big, small, or run away and get married, but know that my pack is excited that you are and want us to be married. The pack wants to share the day with us," Alpha Maximus says.

"I can agree to that if we can get married soon, and I don't mean months from now. I mean next week," I say.

Alpha Maximus turns all his focus to me. "You are ready, now?" he asks.

I nod. "Yes. I kept putting it off because I was afraid I wouldn't be able to let you touch me and that it was not fair to ask you to marry me and not sleep with you, but now I know I can be your lover and your wife," I spill my heart to him. I begin to cry like an idiot. My Alpha, with a hard cock, is between my legs, and I am crying.

Alpha Maximus wipes my tears away. "We can have a ceremony here, just the two of us, and a bigger one later. Would that make you happy?" he asks me.

I smile. "Yes, tomorrow, make me your wife, but tonight please me," I say, pulling him close and forcing his cock to slide into me. I moan as he bottoms out inside me.

The next day Beta Zion married us in a private ceremony. We made a pack announcement and planned a big wedding in six months. This also gives Beta Rocky and Amy a chance to have their big wedding without us taking the shine off their special day.

"To be loved by a wolf is special. No one can interfere when there is true love between a wolf and his mate," Alpha Maximus said as he slid the ring on my finger.

He promised me peace, and in the end, he gave me peace.

THE END

Don't miss out!

Visit the website below and you can sign up to receive emails whenever Lillith Mykals Kennedy publishes a new book. There's no charge and no obligation.

https://books2read.com/r/B-A-LYON-FWGDC

Connecting independent readers to independent writers.

Did you love *The Alpha's Broken Luna*? Then you should read *The Alpha Affair*[1] by Lillith Mykals Kennedy!

Alpha Kai has no intention of choosing a mate. He prefers taking a different woman to his bed every night. Things are going great for the Dark Moon Wolf Pack until he gets a call from Alpha Jake from the Red River Pack. He has a problem with two of his warriors and needs to relocate one. Alpha Kai can always use another warrior. The new wolf Beta Finn has a wife, Alaska, and she is the woman of Alpha Kai's dreams. Alpha Kai wants Alaska to be his mate, and he will stop at nothing to have her.

---

1. https://books2read.com/u/m2drxO

2. https://books2read.com/u/m2drxO

Also by Lillith Mykals Kennedy

The Alpha's Caged Pet
The Alpha's Caged Pet Book 2
The Alpha's Caged Pet

The Alpha's Virgin Slave
The Alpha's Virgin Slave Book 5 The Weeping Wolf

The Vampire Authority
I Belong to a Wolf
The Auction

Standalone
Dirty Little Secret
Flames In The Fire
Her Obsession
The Alpha's Fairy
The Auction Series
The Fairy Vampire Queen

The Imperial Wolves
Hybrid Mates
The Lotus
The Alpha's Virgin Slave Book 1-5
Saved By The Alpha
The Alpha Affair
My Alpha Billionaire Dom
The Alpha's Virgin Vampire Mate
The Devil's Playground
The Devil's Work
Hidden Magic
The Alpha's Broken Luna